JUPITER'S EYE
April 2025

Features
67 *A Stop At Willoughby* Exposes the Horror Possible in the Male Role and in Foolish Nostalgia by Denise Noe
97 Who's Who

Novelettes
10 Uncle Ty's Army
76 Breathing Real Air by Casey Richards-Bradt

Short Stories
44 Sponged by James Dick

Poems
39 Shepherds by Yuliia Vereta

THE STAFF OF JUPITER'S EYE

EDITOR: Tyree Campbell
WEBMASTER: H David Blalock
COVER DESIGNERS: Marcia A. Borell, Laura Givens

All rights reserved. No part of this book may be reproduced or transmitted in any form or by any means, electronic or mechanical, including photocopying or recording or by any information storage and retrieval systems, without expressed written consent of the authors and/or artists.

Jupiter's Eye is a work of fiction. Names, characters, places, and incidents are products of the authors' imaginations. Any resemblance to actual events or persons, living or dead, is entirely coincidental.

Story and illustration copyrights owned by the respective authors.

First Printing April 2025
Hiraeth Publishing
http://hiraethsffh.com/
@HiraethPublish1

Cover art by Richard E. Schell
Cover design by Marcia A. Borell

Vol. I, No. 1   April 2025

Jupiter's Eye is published three times a year on the 1st days of April, August, and December in the United States of America by Hiraeth Publishing, P.O. Box 1248, Tularosa, NM, 88352. Copyright 2025 by Hiraeth Publishing. All rights revert to authors and artists upon publication except as noted in selected individual contracts. Writers and artists guidelines are available online at www.hiraethsffh.com. Guidelines are also available upon request from Hiraeth Publishing, P.O. Box 1248, Tularosa, NM, 88352, if request is accompanied by a self-addressed * * *10 envelope with a first-class US stamp. Editor: Tyree Campbell.

A Little Help, Please

In the world of the small indie press we fight a never-ending battle for attention to our work, as writers and in publishing. Here's an example: big publishers [you know who they are] have gobs of $$$ that they can devote to advertising and marketing. Here at Hiraeth Publishing, our advertising budget consists of the deposits for whatever soda bottles and aluminum cans we can find alongside the highways. Anti-littering laws make our task even more difficult . . . ☺

That's where YOU come in. YOU are our best promoter. YOU are the one who can tell others about us. Just send 'em to our website, tell them about our store. That's all. Just that.

Of course, we don't mind if you talk us up. We're pretty good, you know. We have some award-winning and award-nominated writers and artists, plus other voices well-deserving to be heard [not everyone wins awards, right?] but our publications are read-worthy nevertheless.

That number once again is:
www.hiraethsffh.com

Friend us on Facebook at Hiraeth Publishing
Follow us on Twitter at @HiraethPublish1

Annae (real name Maryjade) is an assassin sent to Deege, a forested world, to kill a plant and bring back the druzy who carries it. Druzies resemble young girls, but seem to have no life and no purpose but to act as transportation to the plants. In the process, Annae loses contact with her own spacecraft and is marooned on the world.

The man who hired Annae for this task is also responsible for the death of Annae's twin sister. Annae has accepted this contract because it presents an opportunity to kill the killer. However, the loss of the twin has crippled Annae. She is virtually unable to communicate with anyone, except in the course of negotiating her contracts. She has taken to talking with the memory of her dead sister, and with no one else.

Now, marooned on Deege, she must find a way to break out of her isolation and communicate with the druzies, and with a strange young woman who cannot speak, or she will be compelled to remain on this world forever.

https://www.hiraethsffh.com/product-page/becoming-jade-by-tyree-campbell

The Sisterhood of the Blood Moon
By Terrie Leigh Relf

For thousands of Earth years, the Transgalactic Consortium has had an invested interest in this planet and its inhabitants, the Haurans. While the Sisterhood of the Blood Moon and the Guardians work together with the Consortium and Haurans to restore balance to the universe, the Blood Moon is fast approaching. The power of this moon reveals untold secrets . . . including the sacred covenant with the Mora Spiders. There is an ancient pact that continues to be honored – but at what cost and for whose purpose?

The world may come to an end. But will there be a chance for a new beginning? And if so, where?

https://www.hiraethsffh.com/product-page/sisterhood-of-the-blood-moon-by-terrie-leigh-relf

INDIGO
By Tyree Campbell

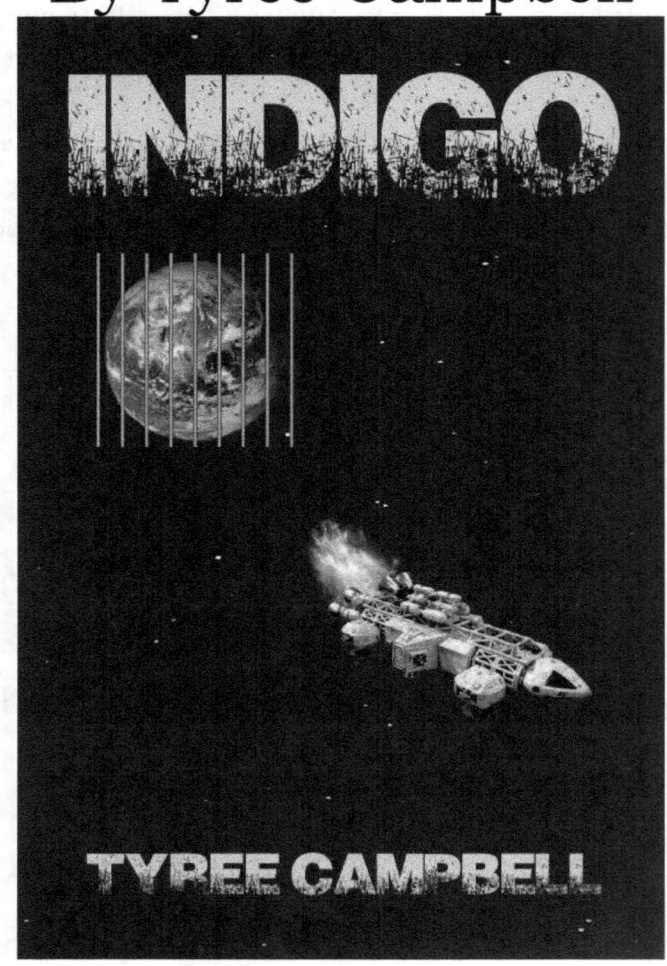

Matt has a special gift that will enable him to avenge his brother's death. Kerise has another use for that talent, if only she can persuade him to abandon his personal quest and help her with a project called Indigo.

Echelon, a secret government project, also wants Matt because of his gift. But as he and other like him cannot be controlled, they pose a threat to national security. Orders go out to have them eliminated.

Interpol is on the lookout for Kerise and for the Indigo project. There is no place on Earth where Matt and Kerise and her associates will be safe. Nowhere on Earth…but they cannot be safe unless Matt commits himself to Indigo. And he's not about to do that…

https://www.hiraethsffh.com/product-page/indigo-by-tyree-campbell

Uncle Ty's Army
David Castlewitz

Leaving the cavernous factory where he worked with his father, Arnie Gross glanced back over his shoulder for one final look at the words emblazoned in large block letters above the double-wide doors: "No Bots, Just Hands." At age 20, he'd been an apprentice for more than two years, working under the supervision of his father, the chief millwright. But Arnie didn't want to take the next step and earn his journeyman's patch. He wanted to leave Middleset, the rural village where he lived.

"I don't need your permission," Arnie told his father.

Ken Gross stopped, hands in the pockets of his grease-stained canvas trousers. Arnie absorbed his dad's narrowed eyes, the hawk-like face that spelled disapproval. He'd seen it all his life, but he was no longer a child who cowered before the master of the house.

"You know what that sign means?" Ken pointed to where Arnie had been looking. "Not like the city factories. No automation. None. That's something to be proud of."

"It's not for me."

"Your Uncle Ty – he's not so great, Arnie."

"You never liked him."

"It's not an army," Dad said. "It's just a street gang. He makes money selling protection. You think he's helping people? He's not."

"I'll make up my own mind."

"Your mom put this idea in your head, didn't she?"

Arnie didn't reply, but Dad was right. Gloria Gross spoke well of her big brother. She protected him when he needed a place to hide. She defended his reputation whenever her husband denigrated him.

"He's got nothing to do with the big factories, Dad."

"He's got everything to do with what's wrong out there. I know. I was born in a group house. My parents were slacks – wasters, unemployed -- living on the government guaranteed wage. The dole."

Arnie had heard this before. After Dad's parents left the group house -- for reasons that were never clear – they lived in a homeless encampment. At age 12, Ken Gross ran off and found Middleset, which took him in. He went to school, lived in a shelter with other kids, and learned mechanics through an on-the-job training program. He never knew what happened to his parents, but assumed they died during the violent crackdowns on encampments and urban shelters. Or they starved to death, he once mused. Or were killed in the riots.

"Don't know, don't care," he often said, especially when he got into an expansive mood and Arnie sat nearby, eager to listen. "I know I made the right choice. I lived."

The problem with the life Ken Gross chose, Uncle Ty said during one of his visits, was how insular rural residents had become. They withdrew from city life, even from life in the suburbs, choosing to live apart from everything except surrounding hamlets and small towns. What they fashioned in their factories and grew on their farms stayed in their communities, their economies limited to what could be locally produced and consumed. They even had their own currency, funded insurance companies to protect homes, and eschewed the national banking system.

In school, teachers praised village life as the best life, defamed the cities as rife with chaos and crime, and taught their students to love and obey the elders of the community. Tell Dad that he wanted something else? Arnie kept trying, but maybe, he thought, he didn't have the right words. Words he'd never find. So, he'd just act.

They turned onto a narrow path between two houses and continued walking until the houses swallowed them. Twilight lent a soft veneer to the day's end and in the distance the scuffling of feet along with shouted commands signaled the assembly of the home guard that protected the hamlet from outsiders, vandals, and roaming gangs.

Dad continued to mumble his complaints about his brother-in-law. Arnie barely listened. It reminded him of his junior year in high school when Miss Sally, a social studies teacher, would rave about the Austerity Years. They ruined her family, by which she meant the other 30-some-year-olds she lived with in a group house.

Word Salad Sally, students called her. She blamed everything on those bad years when food prices rocketed, foreclosures soared, homelessness ... Miss Sally went on and on about the past, blaming her own woeful condition, which included teaching in a village school, on what happened twenty years ago. A middle-aged woman, she sat cross-legged on her desk and preached. She didn't return the next year.

Once home, Arnie found that his mother had kept her promise to contact her brother. While dad visited the adjoining washroom to scrub away the day's grime, Arnie stood in the front room with its flower print covered chairs and mismatched tables and greeted the visitor he'd hoped to see.

"Lindsay Stevens," the visitor said, rising from a deep armchair. Dressed in black, her shirt not tucked into her billowing trousers, she didn't look as military as Arnie thought she should. Even her boots were wrong. They had thick high heels and pointed toes. The woman herself didn't look tough. Too pretty. Blonde hair too long – down to her shoulders.

Uncle Ty hadn't sent her, Arnie feared, but then perked up when he heard the young woman bark an order.

"We leave tonight. After dinner." She handed him a small backpack. "Take what fits and what you think you'll need."

"I'll help," Mom said.

Lindsay shook her head. "He'll do it. You're not going to be there to help him anymore."

Dad walked in, shirt off and flung over one shoulder. No doubt he'd seen Lindsay when he first came home. "I've already put in my opinion," he said, and walked into the next room, where he sat at the table.

"Soup's on the buffet and there's a plate of mixed veggies," Gloria called to her husband.

Arnie heard a grumbled complaint. Dad hated these meals where he just helped himself. Suddenly, he felt tears behind his eyes. He'd miss this. He'd miss the warmth of this large house with its wood paneled walls and heating coils in the floor, the repartee between his parents, and even the fierce eruptions of anger that occurred now and then.

"Give him the exam," Lindsay said with a glance in Gloria's direction.

She nodded. "Strip down, Arnie."

"Mom!"

"Hey," Lindsay snapped. "She's the camp nurse and you're a recruit. Do what you're told."

Later, after a quick dinner, Arnie made his goodbyes. He hugged his mother and shook his father's hand but without looking into his disapproving face.

"We've got a walk ahead of us," Lindsay said.

"How many kids you taking this time?" Ken Gross asked.

"Recruiting, not taking," Lindsay corrected. "There's two other boys and a girl. So, we've got four recruits."

"Do I know any of them?" Arnie asked.

"If you do, keep that to yourself," Lindsay snapped. "Making friends – or keeping them – isn't something you'll want to do."

"Tell my brother – " Gloria didn't complete the sentence.

"Yeah," Lindsay said. "I understand. I'll tell him, but you know how Mr. Tyson is. No favorites."

Gloria wetted her lips and stepped aside. She stood closer to her husband. Arnie led the way out of the house into the moonless night.

"Don't get too far ahead of me," Lindsay said. "I can't see in the dark."

Arnie grinned. He had one up on her. He couldn't see in the dark either, but he was accustomed to these paths between the houses. The crunch of stone under his feet juxtaposed with the soft feel of grass told him where he was going and where he'd just been.

When Lindsay caught up to him, she pulled something from a pouch hanging from her belt.

"There's patrols," Arnie said. "I wouldn't use a flashlight."

"Listen, recruit. Learn this right now. Never correct a superior. Even if you're right."

Arnie chuckled, which he regretted when Lindsay slapped his cheek.

"Shut up. You act like this when we get to the city and you'll go home." She pointed the device ahead of them, consulting the watch on her left wrist, and then settling on a direction. With a perfunctory, "This way," she led Arnie to a parked van.

Inside, a girl and two boys sat in the rear seat, a padded bench. Arnie didn't know any of them. They were young. The girl didn't look to be 20, the minimum age for volunteers. The two boys were tall and skinny, and with that distraught look of hunger Arnie often saw amongst the hamlet's poor.

Lindsay gave orders. No talking. No moving around. Absolutely no attempt to peek outside.

At the hamlet's main gate, the van slowed to a stop. After a good-natured exchange between the driver and the guards, the vehicle moved onto the road. It soon picked up speed, jostling the passengers. Rumbling along, veering left and then right, Arnie guessed they were on a back road cutting through the woods.

The van stopped for a second time. The passenger-side doors opened and Arnie climbed out from the middle seat. He refrained from reaching back to help the girl, guessing the recruiter wouldn't approve.

Lindsay stood in a circle of light from a hand-held lamp, a finger to her lips. One by one, they lined up. She spent a few seconds looking at them, shaking her head, lips pursed. Arnie didn't know why she showed such disapproval, though he guessed the ragged lineup had something to do with it.

Lindsay walked toward a half-buried house set against a small hill. Just the door and a single window were above ground. The rest was nestled in the earth.

"You first," Lindsay said to the girl. "Green door."

Minutes later, Arnie was pointed to that door as well. He didn't hesitate. He walked inside the house, down a ramp and into a room that instantly reminded him of a dentist's office with its white walls and beeping monitors.

Two men in white lab coats stood by a padded chair. Arnie followed their silent instructions and positioned himself face down in a prone position. He didn't like feeling a strap over his waist, but guessed it was to hold him steady.

Then came a pinch at the back of his skull, near the nape of his neck.

"That's so the next part doesn't hurt," someone said.

"You going to tell me what's going to happen?" Arnie asked.

"Didn't Miss Lindsay tell you not to ask questions?"

Arnie didn't reply. Numbness spread across the back of his neck. A dull ache came next. The ping of something metallic dropping into an aluminum tray chimed near his face. Out of the corner of one eye he saw a red-hot circle, and then a sharp pain touched his neck.

One of the men released the strap holding him down and helped him to sit up. Arnie took a towel from him and pressed it against the wound in his neck. He checked for blood. None on the white towel. The cauterizing pen did a good job of sealing the cut. A red puddle in a tray on a cart next to the chair grabbed his attention.

"That's your tracker," one of the two men said.

The bloody half inch-long cylinder that had been in his body since childhood had never been an issue for him, though his father often railed against the government's practice of tracking its citizens with the device. No doubt, Uncle Ty didn't want his recruits on anyone's radar.

"There's a box just past that door. Change your clothes. Lindsay'll come get you when she's ready."

Later, after more than an hour of sitting in silence with the other recruits, Lindsay appeared. She held a plastic case that contained four glass vials, each with a metal cylinder inside. No blood, so they must've been cleaned.

"We save these," she said. "If you get sent back, you get chipped again."

Arnie had no intention of being sent back. He didn't want to disappoint his mother. He didn't want to give Dad anything to use against him in the future. Being part of Uncle Ty's army was something he'd always wanted. Now he was dressed in billowing black trousers and a black shirt a size too big, the long sleeves rolled up past his wrists. Thick faux-leather boots replaced the loafers he'd been wearing. A cloth cap with no brim covered his head. The back of his shirt collar rubbed at his neck, where a gnawing pain intensified when the anesthetic wore off.

* * *

After two weeks of climbing walls, running the track in the 20th floor gym carved out of an office building Uncle Ty's army had taken over, and squirming through tunnels in the basement, Arnie welcomed the chance to get outside. The city air stung his eyes, but the old hands, men and women who'd served Tyson for years, weren't bothered by it, and Arnie assumed he'd eventually acclimatize himself.

He stood outside a liquor store that was well lit on the inside, though dark outside, where damaged streetlamps provided none of the light that bathed nearby streets. Along this block, boarded up storefronts evidenced a past when shops and boutiques proliferated. Now, the two-story brick buildings stood mostly abandoned, with a convenience store at the corner and this liquor store in the middle. The clerks in those places probably served their customers from behind bars and heavy-duty glass.

As his mother once told him, things like cities didn't die all at once. They were like potted plants that slowly withered but didn't just topple over one day. Leaves died. Stems decayed. The roots rotted. No single event killed them.

He stared at an abandoned supermarket across the street and wondered how many squatters lived there. As he thought about it, he realized he hadn't seen any robotaxis. For that matter, there weren't any potential customers. The streets were empty, though he noticed a one-car tram pass a block away, its trolley sparking against the overhead wires. He guessed it was autonomous because he'd ridden it once six years ago when his father attended a convention of community directors and brought him along, so he could see that life was better in the village. An armed guard rode where a driver would've been seated and registered customers' fares.

Dad left the city when the convention dissolved into chaos. He didn't explain why, other than to complain that some people wanted to take more than they gave. From what Arnie learned, the decaying city wanted to tax the surrounding farms and hamlets and towns, incorporate them, and take advantage of their largess.

Arnie shook his head to wipe away the thoughts crowding his mind. He'd once heard Uncle Ty claim that the urban landscape could be resurrected, that it wouldn't belong to the lucky few, the slicks – those with jobs -- who lived in gated communities or impenetrable high-rises or the slackers in their group houses. Small shops would proliferate. Outlying farms that served the villages would once again send their produce into the city, set up markets, and not worry about food riots destroying their livelihoods. Eliminate automation, rid the factories of robots, stop the guaranteed wage, and give everyone a job. Revive self-pride. Rebuild what was broken. Repair the rift between urban and rural. Ty's three "R's."

People were meant to contribute to society, not live off it. Sometimes, Arnie thought, Dad and Uncle Ty agreed about things. But Dad always left the room in disgust when Ty preached his beliefs, mumbling that Ty was part of the problem, not the solution; Mom gushed with pride in her brother. Recalling these scenes made Arnie smile.

"Pay attention. All of you."

Arnie winced. Had he looked like he'd been dreaming? Worse, napping? One of several recruits – newts – among the squad of old hands, he was armed with a three-foot-long flexible metal club like everyone else.

Was this a training exercise or a real assignment? He knew not to ask anyone. Not Mr. Henry, their instructor, or even the old hands.

Of the three newts Arnie had been with when he left home, one – the young girl – had already been discharged. She lasted a week before Hank – Mr. Henry to you, Arnie had been warned – sent her away. Arnie suspected it was because she asked too many questions.

Glancing up, he noticed a flickering electric lamp in the store's alcove between the display windows. An old-fashioned black-and-white tiled walkway led to a formidable steel door covered by wire mesh. Two young men, one with freckles, and neither of them looking at all like army types, huddled by the door, each with a plastic box in his lap. They fiddled with knobs and toggle switches. One – Freckles -- raised an antenna.

Mr. Henry said, "Keep alert, newts."

At the end of the street, a small group had assembled. Arnie knew there was rioting that erupted in the city, often with no real cause, spurred on by politics, food scarcity, and the heat of summer, the cold of winter. His uncle made most of his money providing guard services and protection. This is what this was, he assured himself. They'd been sent to guard the liquor store, often the rioters' favorite target.

The shadowy group at the end of the street took on the distinct shape of ten men carrying chains, brass knuckles, and baseball bats. Something on a lamp post beeped and blinked red. Motion detector? They were all over the factory where he'd worked. Dad often repaired or replaced the outdoor units, which got clobbered during the winter storms.

He had to get Dad out of his head!

He concentrated on the advancing gang. Looking up and down the line of men and women in front of him, he made a quick count. Eight old hands. Six trainees. Good. They outnumbered the other gang.

Someone up ahead barked, "Ready up!" And the opposing men broke into a run.

Mr. Henry shouted orders, but Arnie didn't hear him over the clamor of the fighting that erupted. Clubs clashed. Fists and knives met one another with a ferocity that Arnie had never seen before. There were plenty of fights at school. There was fighting sometimes at the factory. But seeing two gangs clash like this...

While his fellow newts stepped forward to engage anyone who got past the front line, Arnie stumbled. He didn't raise his club until he heard two shots ring out. One of the attackers dropped onto the asphalt. The rest turned and ran while the old hands cheered and shook their fists at them. Arnie's fellow trainees congratulated one another, laughing and smiling and fist-bumping.

Surprisingly, there was no blood on the ground.

"You froze, Gross," Mr. Henry said.

Arnie didn't reply. He'd only been a step or two late getting into the fight.

The attacker on the ground, the one who'd been shot, stood up and wiped his hands on his pants.

"Good job, Deke," an old hand called out. The "wounded" attacker waved and lopped down the street.

A training exercise? Arnie gaped at the scene.

Someone ran toward the store from the alley. "Maties coming. Maties."

"Alright," Mr. Henry shouted. "There's a van up the block."

"We got this," the freckle-faced boy said as he worked the knobs arrayed across the front of the plastic box in his lap.

Two seven-foot-tall cop-bots emerged from an intersecting street alongside the shuttered supermarket. They twisted their metallic heads in a wide arc, their spindly legs bent at the knees and their arms straight at their sides.

"They changed the pass phrase," Freckles said. "Damn. Changed it just as I – "

The old hands were already sprinting up the street, in the direction of where the "attackers" had come. Arnie followed, along with everyone else except Freckles. But then he, too, stood up and raced away while the robots stomped along the sidewalk,

An old hand named Jay plopped down in the alcove when everyone else ran for the van. When Arnie stopped and looked back, Jay was dousing himself with something in a bottle.

"Don't worry about him," one of the old hands said, grabbing Arnie by the shoulder and pointing him toward the end of the street. "He'll give the maties something to check out. An old drunk smelling of booze. They won't have time to get to us."

"Had to be the shots," Freckles said under his breath as he sprinted past. "That brought them out. That's why they changed pass phrases."

His companion disagreed. "They detected you trying to get in."

Arnie clambered into the waiting van. He reached back and helped Freckles climb onto the bumper at the back door.

"What're you trying to do with that?" Arnie asked, pointing at the box in Freckle's hands.

Instead of an answer, Arnie got a cold look. Not just from the freckle-faced boy with the box or his companion, who had a similar device, but also from the old hands. Nobody liked to answer questions. Arnie chided himself for asking.

The van progressed smoothly on the paved street, its electric motor humming. They turned into a tunnel leading to an underground garage. With no windows in the back of the van and his view of the windshield obscured by a screen separating the passenger section from the driver's, Arnie had little idea of where he was. While he lived and trained in an abandoned 25 story tall office building, its exact location in the city was kept from him. It was just one of many such buildings in which squatters took up residence. The police, he'd been told, seldom bothered squatters. They protected the wealthier parts of the city.

"Don't go nowhere," Mr. Henry said after Arnie filed out of the van in the garage. While everyone else headed for the elevator, Arnie remained behind.

"You froze, didn't you?"

Arnie heard his father yelling at him. *Don't back down. Never back off.* That's what Dad said when Arnie complained of bullying at school or feeling out of place at the factory.

"I didn't freeze. I didn't even hesitate. I tripped. I started to get into the fight, but then – Hell, Mr. Henry, it was all a training thing anyway."

"You froze. That's going to be in my report. Now, be smart and stop arguing."

Arnie closed his mouth, swallowing any retort he might make, and not really knowing what else he could say.

"Expect a couple of weeks of extra duty, kid. That'll teach you to freeze up."

Arnie hurried out of Mr. Henry's sight, into the elevator, happy to have only gotten a stint of extra duty. He didn't want to be expelled.

* * *

Curious, Arnie aimed his broom toward the large table in the middle of the room, sweeping as he went, the roving vacuum cleaner behind him collecting the piles of debris he left in his wake. Circuit boards, small white trays full of parts, and spools of wire covered the tabletop. A small wave-soldering machine flashed green, and Freckles pulled out a finished board, blew on it, and inspected it. His companion, the other old hand who'd been at the liquor store, typed furiously on a click-clacking keyboard, his face close to a flat screen monitor.

Freckles looked up and Arnie caught his eye. "You're one of Hank's screw ups," Freckles said.

Arnie blushed. "He's Mr. Henry to me," he said, and grinned, hoping Freckles would suddenly be friendly.

"Don't badger the kid," the other boy said. Arnie bristled. Kid? These two didn't look any older than him.

"Sweep up crew, huh?" Freckles said.

Arnie nodded. Last week he'd been on kitchen duty for both the midnight breakfast served to late night crews and morning breakfast that everyone else attended. He still had to report for the afternoon training sessions, so he hadn't had much sleep.

"Know anything about electronics?" the other boy at the table asked. He slid off his stool and extended his hand. "Quincy."

Arnie introduced himself, wondering if Quincy was a first name or a last. He told himself to be satisfied that he'd been introduced at all.

"He's a borough kid," Freckles said. "What's he know?"

"You're right," Arnie said. "I don't know. Maybe I'd like to find out. I'm a fast learner."

Freckles laughed.

Quincy looked askance at his teammate, and then turned back to Arnie. "We're trying to disrupt the maties. Get into their programming."

"What're maties?" Arnie asked, thinking of those tall skinny robots encountered near the liquor store. "The robots?"

"Yeah," Freckles said.

Quincy chuckled. "Somebody yelled 'Come on, Maties" once or twice to get the robots to attack us. I think it was one of the cops. Anyway, the term stuck, especially when the news media picked it up. You never heard it before?"

Not in the borough, Arnie thought. There was little city news at home. No television broadcasts – no TV monitors for that matter – and home radios were limited. Dad had one because he served on the village board of directors, but he kept it in a locked drawer. It was something Arnie lived with, so he didn't think it unusual. City news, he was told multiple times, was never good news. His home village produced its own eight-page newspaper, a form of media missing in the cities, where news was distributed online by a single entity. The village paper reported local events and that of nearby communities. What happened in the cities stayed there.

"It's not easy," Freckles said. "Getting into their data stream. Then turning them around or doing something to stop them from charging. That's the idea. Understand?"

Arnie did. That's what they meant about the changing pass phrase. Freckles had the phrase, but it changed a second later and left him with no control over the robots.

"So, you're figuring out why the pass phrase changed, right?" Arnie said.

Quincy pursed his thin lips and nodded, his floppy brown hair drooping over his forehead and covering his eyes.

"You got it," Freckles said.

"Good luck with that," Arnie said. He returned to sweeping, to staying ahead of the meandering vacuum cleaner. He didn't want to overstay his welcome, but this piqued his interest. "How'd you learn this stuff? Tech school?"

"Me?" Quincy said. "Yeah. Two years. Then got froze out afterwards. Test scores not high enough."

Freckles volunteered, "Some slick – you know, a guy with a good job – was brought in to teach the fundamentals. Because Ty had this idea to disrupt the cop-bots."

Quincy chimed in with, "A slick who lost his job to automation."

"Didn't know that could happen," Arnie said. Bots in the factories were common, which put a lot of people out of work. But he'd heard his father complain that teachers, doctors, and other professionals were replaced as well. Hearing about this engineer confirmed Dad's complaints. It made village life look better. But Uncle Ty wanted to do for the city what others did for the rural, starting with the cop-bots.

"We use coding bots," Quincy said. "For some stuff. No way around it."

Freckles shook his head. "A sad fact."

A woman barged into the room. "You got that simulation ready?" She glared at Arnie and added, "You can clean some other time. Mr. Tyson's on his way for a demo."

Arnie backed off, feeling like he'd just been scolded. Like his mother, the woman who'd just entered was short and matronly, her graying hair smothered under netting. Dressed in a crisp black uniform, pants sharply creased, and blouse tucked in, she possessed a true military look.

Quickly, Arnie headed to the door. In all these weeks he had yet to see his uncle, and now Ty was on his way. Should he linger near the elevator bank just so he could say hello? Maybe it was better to slink away.

Arnie stopped at a stairwell, eyes on the elevator doors. They opened and two black-clad men stepped out of the car. They were followed by a tall heavyset man with a crop of thick blonde hair combed straight back from a high forehead. He glanced sideways and so did the other two men. Arnie flinched when he realized all eyes were on him. He wondered if he was expected to salute.

"Uncle Ty," he whispered, the salutation escaping from him before he even thought of it.

"That's Mr. Tyson to you," his uncle snapped, and took several long strides to the open door into the electronics lab. The sharply dressed matronly woman poked her head out from inside the room.

"Better get out of here," she said before shutting the door.

Arnie fled down the stairwell without looking back, without asking "Why?"

* * *

Nervous, Arnie slowed his pace as he walked down the cement stairs to the sub-basement. Trainees weren't allowed to use the elevators except when on duty or punishment detail, so he'd taken the steps starting at his sixth-floor dormitory, eager to see his uncle, yet dreading the prospect as he neared Ty's office.

A virtual assistant occupied a small table in the anteroom. Its image was of an older woman who looked like someone from a vintage 20th century viddie, like the ones shown in the dayroom on a wall-mounted flat screen, a rare treat that Arnie enjoyed. Gray hair. Polka dot dress. Lined face and beady eyes.

"Sit and wait," the virtual said with a wave of her hand, which sported a jeweled ring on the little finger.

Arnie sat. He had only another hour before reporting to the cafeteria for the midnight breakfast shift. This was the start of his third week on the punishment detail, with assignments ranging from sweep-up to KP to latrine duty. He liked none of it.

"Okay, Arnie," Tyson said, one large hand on the open door and the other clamped against the side of the wall. "Come on in."

Arnie walked between his uncle and the door frame, head down. He sat in one of the three green swivel office chairs in front of Tyson's desk and glanced at the empty walls, the empty desktop, and the bare cement floor.

"I guess you know not to call me Uncle Ty when people are around. Don't do it when people aren't around either. Bad for morale. Yours, I mean. Okay? I know what your father thinks of this outfit, but it's not some ragtag gang. We're an important part of the community."

"Sorry, Mr. Tyson. I'll make sure I don't slip up."

Tyson didn't smile. A tiny tic appeared at the corner of his mouth. It pulsed, and thin blue lines emanated outwards into his sunken cheeks.

"Hank says you froze on a mission."

Arnie shook his head. "I stumbled a bit, so it looked like I hesitated." He'd mentally reviewed the incident several times. Though he didn't jump into the fight, he didn't freeze; he tripped over something on the sidewalk.

Tyson squinted at his hands, which were folded together and resting against the edge of the desk. "What can you do for us?" he asked. "Training's almost over. Is there some special skill you can offer?"

"I just want to be useful."

Tyson nodded. The tic disappeared. He stopped squinting. "Hank isn't so sure you won't screw up before training's over."

Arnie swallowed. "I won't."

"Cole and Quincy thought you had an interest in what they do," Tyson said.

Cole? That must be Freckles' name. "I didn't understand any of it," Arnie said with a soft laugh. "But, yeah, it's interesting."

"Well, we'll see. They do important work here."

"Did the demo go like you wanted?" Arnie ventured, hoping he hadn't stepped out of line by asking such a direct question.

"Some of it. Now we need to test it RL. Real life. You know?"

Arnie nodded.

"Basically, we need bait to attract the police and their – their things."

"Maties?" Arnie offered.

Tyson snorted, his nostrils quivering. "I hate that term, but, yeah, that's what we're after."

"Anything I can do to help?" Arnie sensed his uncle leading up to asking, so he decided to offer it first.

Tyson opened a desk drawer and pulled out a palm-sized plastic box. He opened it and drew out a glass cylinder. Arnie recognized its contents. The vial held someone's tracker, like the one taken out of the back of his neck.

"The plan is to plant someone in an empty building. There's dozens in the city. Decrepit old places that even squatters don't like."

Arnie waited to hear more.

Tyson continued. "The police pick up the tracker's signal and move in."

"For just one person?"

"There'll be a threat posted on the *ThisHere* site. The police monitor the city-wide online forums."

Arnie had only read about forums and online communities. Those things were forbidden in the boroughs.

"The cops will think whoever's in this building alone isn't just some squatter, but someone about to plant a bomb."

Arnie nodded. He understood.

"You'll be on the second or third floor. The rest of the team will be either right above or just below, depending on which building we pick. They don't have trackers, so they won't be picked up. For wherever they're posted, in whatever room they wait, there'll be a screen across all the windows to block infrared so there's no heat registers, just like we use here." Tyson waved at the ceiling, as though to indicate all the floors above his basement lair.

"And when the police and the cop-bots – the maties -- arrive?" Arnie asked, excited to be conspiring with his uncle.

"Quincy and Cole will turn them against the cops."

Arnie pictured a massacre.

"We're not out to kill anyone," Tyson quickly added. "Just... confuse things. You'll get out. Someone will help you. Through a vent or something. We'll nail down the details once we pick a site."

Arnie nodded again.

"Your tracker has to go back in," Tyson said. "That okay with you?"

"Absolutely." Arnie sprung to his feet. "When do I get started?"

"I'll keep Hank up-to-date, and he'll put you in the loop at the right time. Until then ... " Tyson bit his lower lip. His tic re-appeared. "Keep doing what you're told and don't get on Hank's bad side."

* * *

The medic who reinserted Arnie's tracker wasn't as adept at his job as the one who operated on him the first time. There'd not been a shot to dull the pain. There'd been a topical and he'd been given some pills, but he felt every cut and pull of the flesh when the tracker went back in.

Nauseous after the procedure, Arnie needed help getting to the car waiting to take him to -- *wherever*. So far, he'd been put into a whirlwind of activity, starting with being pulled from a detail helping put protective boards over store windows on a wide avenue frequented by mostly poor shoppers. Some politician – Arnie didn't know which one because he didn't pay much attention to the news – promised a huge weekend rally in support of a cost-of-living increase to the monthly guaranteed income. Looting could be expected, so Tyson's army prepared for action, promising paying clients there'd be a squad to protect their businesses as well as their lives.

Stuffed under blankets in the back seat, Arnie settled in for a ride that proved to be much shorter than he'd anticipated. In just a few minutes he was ushered out of the car. Freckles draped a mesh covering over Arnie's head, explaining that it dampened the tracker's signal, though it wasn't 100 percent effective.

Brick walls, thick wooden timbers, and high ceilings reminded Arnie of the factory in the borough where he'd worked with his dad. Several long rows of huge cement vats spoke in eerie whispers of a bygone urban industry. Cables and large spools of black insulated wire encrusted with grime and mold littered the floor, along with overturned benches and stools, as well as desks jammed into a corner. A dim light from a single lamp dangling overhead spread a steady glow.

"This place hummed," Freckles said. "Back when. Then they brought in the bots, and it was one human to two mechanicals. Now it's one guy to forty. That's what big factories are like. These old places just went to rot." He spoke that last part with distaste, then spat as though to emphasize his words.

Arnie resisted the urge to shrug or even to nod, not knowing what was expected. He'd been told that automation brought back manufacturing. All sorts of products that were once imports were now home grown. Same thing with food. Giant robot-aided farms produced everything from wheat to beans to corn. Little arrived from other countries. Even fisheries came back to life. But every advance was at the cost of human dignity. Too much bad along with the good, his teachers preached.

According to Dad, even the atmospheric "sponges," aerial robots that absorbed carbon dioxide and cleaned the air, were anathema. They didn't need to be automatons; they could be piloted. They could have a crew. People could be put to work flying them. Workers didn't even benefit with jobs building the "sponges."

As the thoughts stormed through Arnie's mind, he couldn't tell if that was Dad speaking or Uncle Ty. Which made him realize, the two men were saying the same thing.

"Walk around," Freckles said. "Or sit. Whatever you want. Wait it out."

"How do I -- ?" Arnie let his question dangle.

"Escape?" Freckles said with a snort. "Don't worry about it. Mr. Tyson's not going to let you get shot up. You're on the second floor. It won't be hard to get out."

Arnie wandered to the cracked and broken windows along one wall. He looked at an empty lot where, he imagined, workers once parked their cars. An elevated light rail system stood on the other side of the lot and a two-car train rumbled along the tracks while he watched.

But there were no people in the nearby streets or in the narrow alleys. No one skulking at the edges of the soft illumination from the streetlights. No patrol cars inching along. No maties – the robot cops – conducting programmed tours. Here and there, light shone in a window of a nearby apartment building.

He waited. He walked some more, counting his footsteps.

Until he heard car doors slamming shut. His heart raced and his breath came in quick jolts.

Back at the windows, Arnie scanned his surroundings for the source of the sounds. He saw nothing, so he hurried to the other side, where there were fewer windows. He scratched away the caked dirt on the glass, spitting and wiping it with his shirt sleeve.

Three-wheeler police cycles stood parked at crazy angles next to the curb. A black van opened its side doors, and several robots piled out, some of them falling forward, their balancing circuits failing them. That brought a smile to Arnie's lips. Everyone liked to see these cop-bots fail, even in some small way.

More vans arrived and more robots filled the street. The cops wore bullet proof vests emblazoned with their precinct number in the back, above the letters "MP" for municipal police. Some had pistols in their hands and others carried short range electronic guns that propelled explosive pellets. Others carried traditional rifles like the kind Arnie saw his dad use when he went hunting. They fired several rounds per second, though his father boasted that he never put his assault rifle in anything but semi-automatic mode.

Now's a good time to get out of here, Arnie mused and wondered about the rescue team. Couldn't just be Freckles and, perhaps, Quincy. And what kind of weapons did the team have? So far, Arnie hadn't seen a single gun at HQ. He guessed there were some. It was an army, wasn't it? Mopping and sweeping made him somewhat invisible and he once overheard a guy bragging about bodyguard duty when "them big honchos got together." Bodyguard? Had to be armed with more than a club.

He gravitated to the room's shadows, thinking of it as a refuge. A useless one though since the robots were equipped with more than common vision. They'd detect his tracker. A police monitor floating above the building had already found him, he assumed. The pounding he heard was either boots coming up the stairs or gloved fists hitting a wall.

He told himself to wait. He was bait.

He stared at the pile of desks and chairs and realized they blocked a door.

Squatting behind a counter, Arnie disturbed a nest of mice. He gasped when the rodents scurried away. They didn't scare him, but he hadn't expected to encounter anything. This refuge wouldn't last, he knew, and soon he'd have to scurry away as well.

The robots burst in, the door flying off its hinges and the barricade of desks and chairs exploding outwards. They advanced and formed a diamond shaped phalanx. They moved in thunderous lock step, and Arnie imagined their beady red eyes penetrating the dark, assembling raw data for analysis.

Then they stopped and their heads swiveled left and right. Cops followed them, shouting. Some of the robots raised the fist-sized rail guns hardwired to their internal circuitry. Pellets exploded against the concrete floor. The police stumbled over one another to get away. Robots fired point-blank at each other. They head-butted. They rammed one another with their bodies.

Arnie looked at the open doorway where he'd entered the room. Two spindly robots stood there, killing his hope of making a dash in that direction.

"This way, kid!"

Arnie took a deep breath. He'd never ever been glad to see Mr. Henry before. Now was the exception.

"Follow me and we'll get out of here."

Arnie walked with his head and knees bent, just as he'd been trained. Mr. Henry often had the recruits waddling around the gym in that position.

Hank steered him to an air vent. Arnie tumbled in. Where the vent shot straight up, a rope ladder dropped, and he climbed to an upper floor. There, a trio of old hands hustled Arnie out of the building and onto a fire escape landing. No cops anywhere, Arnie noted with relief. No bots, either. Just a waiting car, its engine humming.

The old hands jumped off the outside staircase's landing, and Arnie did the same, using the flex-the-knees-and-roll technique he'd been taught just a week or so ago.

Mr. Henry jumped last.

Once in the car, Arnie took his cues from Quincy. Lying on the floor, he adjusted the cover draped over his head. With a lurch, the car darted forward. The driver cursed, complaining that the shade across the window next to him kept peeling at the top corners.

"Press it against the glass," Cole – Freckles -- shouted back. "They'll be checking for heat signatures."

The car's tires screeched. More sharp turns led to a bumpy ride, which soon became smooth and easy on Arnie's body. Relaxed, he melded with the car's slow and rhythmic motion, the engine's hum adding soothing background noise.

Then the car stopped, and he tumbled out. Mr. Henry helped him to his feet. Brushing off imagined dust and dirt from his pants, he looked up at a small dark house surrounded by weeds and bare earth. A cement path led to a narrow porch at the top of several wooden steps. He expected he'd have his tracker removed before going back to HQ.

"Inside," Mr. Henry said with a gentle push. "Careful. The steps."

"I see," Arnie mumbled. He looked forward to rejoining his fellow trainees, but he didn't relish the idea of that inept medic operating on him again.

Tyson came out onto the porch, a screen door banging shut behind him and rattling on its hinges. His huge bulk blocked the light coming from inside the house. A faint halo surrounded his head.

Arnie paused. He hadn't expected to see his uncle. "Did something go wrong?" he asked.

Tyson crooked a finger and opened the screen door. "It worked the way we expected," he said as he ushered Arnie into the house, its front room well-lit by a floor lamp in a corner.

Tyson sat at one end of a long sofa with ripped cushions, the stuffing sticking out everywhere. Two gunmen stood guard at the windows. Arnie glanced at them and tried not to show much interest. These were the first armed guards he'd seen in his many weeks with his uncle's urban army.

"We didn't have time to put up the shades to keep the monitors from sensing our body heat," Tyson explained. "So, we've got a couple of guards in case we need them."

Arnie nodded.

"You did a good job," Tyson said. "Now it's time you went back."

"To training, right?"

"Back to your mom and dad," Tyson said.

"You said I did a good job," Arnie blurted.

"You're not cut out for this. You could get hurt. Get killed. You think I can do that to my sister? Let her son get hurt or killed trying to be what he's not made for? Come on, Arnie. Don't you realize, you're in deeper than you should be."

"I don't realize. I don't want to – "

"My decision's made. You want to be part of this, then do what I say. You can still serve the cause. Talk to your mom. She'll tell you how."

Tyson stood up.

Arnie sat back against the torn cushions. He bit his lower lip.

"After we leave," Tyson said with a wave of his hand that took in the armed guards, "you just go. Let the patrols find you. You've got your tracker. Tell them you ran away from home."

"And you think the cops will believe me?"

"Kids are always running away from the boroughs to see what the city's like."

"This isn't fair."

"It's the way things need to be," Tyson said. He walked into the next room, his guards following behind him. Arnie sat on the edge of the couch, his clasped hands trembling as he held them between his knees.

A woman in a ratty dress, entered the room. "You can't stay here," she said. "I told Mr. Ty – "

"I'm going," Arnie said, and walked out of the house.

* * *

Pain came in waves. Arnie strained against the constraints binding his wrists to a steel chair bolted to the floor. The pain made him wonder if he'd been hit on the head or if he'd fallen and cracked his skull.

The immediate past was a jumble of disjointed images. He recalled standing outside that decrepit house where Uncle Ty gave him the bad news. He remembered the sinking feeling in his bowels when he realized he had to find his way home and admit to his father that he'd failed.

Now, strapped to a chair, wrists bound and a wide belt around his middle, Arnie tried to figure out how he'd gotten into this predicament. He'd walked away from that house, passed other small houses spaced evenly apart on both sides of the street. They all looked occupied, with light peeking out from the edges of curtains across the windows.

And then came a car...

"Awake?"

The voice broke through his attempt at reconstructing what had happened.

"What's going on?" Arnie asked. "You got me tied down and – " A slap across his cheek stopped him. He hadn't seen the hand coming. In the harsh light of a hot lamp on a nearby table an angry face with a bent nose and close-set eyes faced him.

"I ask the questions," the speaker said.

"And I ask them, too," someone else said. That person stood behind Arnie.

Arnie knew what story to tell. He'd picked up on Uncle Ty's prompts, so he easily fabricated a tale to account for being on that residential street, out in public after curfew. He spoke slowly, taking in big gulps of stale air, ignoring the fetid odor that surrounded him.

He'd run away from a rural borough. He wanted to see the city. Now he wanted to get home. It was that simple, he claimed. He just wanted to get home.

"How did you get here?"

Arnie thought for a second. He hadn't anticipated that question, though he knew he should have. "Truck driver. Gave me a lift."

"A truck driver? Not a self-drive? That's unusual."

Arnie answered quickly. "Not on the back roads. We got drivers all the time."

"And you think you'll get a driver to take you back?"

"I don't know," Arnie said. "Maybe I can hop a freight."

The interrogator behind him laughed.

"And maybe you've got a different story," the beady-eyed one said.

"Why're you dressed all in black like that? Like some urban guerrilla."

"I thought it was a good disguise. I thought I'd blend in."

Again, laughter from the one at his back. A shake of the head from the one in front. A third man appeared. He pushed a cart close to Arnie. A smoldering stone brazier on the cart sent irritating tendrils of smoke into the air. This newcomer raked the coals with metal tongs, his hand wrapped in a dark rag. Small sparks flew from the brazier. Using the tongs, he picked up a metal bar that had been lying in the embers.

Arnie flinched. "Cops don't do that," he whimpered.

One of the three said, "How would you know what cops do or don't? You never been in the city before."

"And maybe we're not cops," another said. "Maybe we're freelance. We'll do anything we want to you. Including slit your throat because you're not worth our time."

"What do you want?" Arnie stammered.

"Tells us who you are, where you're from, what you're doing here, and maybe why there's a fresh cut at the back of your neck."

"I don't have a cut," Arnie lied. "You must've done that when you grabbed me off the street."

"Here's the deal, kid. Tell us the truth. If we can sell you to the cops, we will. If you've got nothing – " The statement dangled like a knife over his head.

"I told you," Arnie insisted. Just as he spoke, a searing hot pain struck him. Something pressed against the top of his spine, on the bare flesh just above his shirt collar. The burning sensation spread across his back, through his body and into his bowels. His legs shook. Tears welled in his eyes, then fell on his cheek.

The one with the tongs dropped the white-hot piece of metal back into the brazier and stirred the coals, making sparks fly.

"That's a sample. You got other parts of your body we can burn, and they're more sensitive than your back."

Mouth dry, Arnie couldn't speak.

"You sit there. Think about your story. We'll be back."

The cart was wheeled away, past the glow of the lamp, into the dark. Footsteps behind him and the opening and closing of a door told Arnie that he was alone now. How much more of this could he endure? He had only this story to tell, the one he'd already told. Anything else would betray Uncle Ty, and he didn't want to do that. Besides, he didn't know much. He'd never seen where Ty's HQ was in relation to the rest of the city. Every time he left, it was by car or by van driven out of an underground garage, and his view was always obstructed by shades or a meshed cover over his face.

He wouldn't tell them that. He'd endure what he needed to endure.

Footsteps. Again. Just one person. The beady-eyed guy stood in front of Arnie. "Ready to let us in on your secrets? You think you owe anybody anything, but you don't."

"I told you, I'm just trying to get home."

The one with the brazier, the one who'd burned him, re-appeared. He pushed the cart close. He raked the coals. An acrid smell drifted toward Arnie and wafted across his nose. The smell tickled his nostrils. He stared at the tongs gripping that hot piece of metal. He mentally prepared himself for the pain he knew would be coming. He squeezed his eyes shut.

"Ready to tell the truth?"

"I've told you," Arnie insisted. "The truth. I already told you." He gulped as he watched out of the corner of his eye while the tongs moved toward his back. He cringed. He steeled himself.

"I think he's told us all he can."

Arnie recognized the voice. Uncle Ty stepped in front of him. Mr. Henry stood beside him. Someone removed the strap around his waist and then the bands holding down his wrists.

"What is this?" Arnie blurted. "Another training exercise? They burned my back. Damn, Uncle Ty – Mr. Tyson! Damn." He felt the back of his neck, right above the knob at the top of his spine. It was wet.

The one with the tongs laughed and showed Arnie a bowl of ice cubes.

"Ice?" Arnie asked, amazed.

"Yeah. Show you a hot metal bar and then apply an ice cube to your back, and you don't know the difference. Mind trick."

"Good job," Tyson said. He offered Arnie his hand.

Arnie hesitated, but then clasped his uncle's hand and let himself be pulled to his feet. "Is this what you do to every recruit?"

"Just the ones we like," Mr. Henry said.

* * *

The ceremony reminded Arnie of graduating from school; except he was the only one on stage. None of the other trainees he'd served with over the past few weeks had yet made the grade. They were still in Mr. Henry's charge, still fighting to earn their place. They were still newts.

Many of the old hands sat at the tables placed around the room while the KP squad brought drinks and snacks. Voices rose to a crescendo, some jovial and some argumentative. A stage at one end of the room stood on concrete blocks and the old hands applauded when Arnie walked on. Hank and Tyson joined him.

Conversations stopped. A hush fell over the room. Electric outlets and cables wrapped around evenly spaced posts spoke of a bygone time when this was office space filled with cubicles and desks.

Tyson gave a brief presentation recounting how Arnie helped Cole and Quincy turn the robot cops against one another when they were drawn to investigate the signal of a lone tracker in a building showing several heat signatures.

Mr. Henry told about kidnapping him and the fake interrogation, how they'd fooled him with ice that felt like the pain of white-hot steel.

That inept medic who'd operated on Arnie handed Tyson a small brown paper wrapped package. Arnie had been the guy's victim twice. Once to insert the tracker at the base of his skull and then, immediately after the fake interrogation, to remove it.

"Know what this is?" Tyson unwrapped the package. He held up an inch-long glass cylinder.

Arnie rubbed the back of his neck. "I know."

Old hands chuckled. Arnie guessed many of them had been that medic's victim.

Tyson placed the cylinder on the floor. "There's no going back now."

Arnie smiled. He took Ty's foot stomping motion as a signal. "Understood," he said, and stomped on the tracker in its glass enclosure, destroying the cylinder and its contents.

Applause exploded across the room. Some old hands, including Cole – Freckles – and Quincy came on stage to congratulate Arnie. Even Lindsay appeared. She gave him a brief hug.

"Now you're a nuggie," Mr. Henry said. "New guy."

"So I went from newt to nuggie," Arnie said with a grin. "Does that mean I get to call you Hank?"

Mr. Henry shook his head. "Wait a year for your status to change to old hand. Maybe then."

Arnie accepted that. He looked forward to all the changes that the year would bring. He looked forward to visiting home, perhaps going with his uncle. He looked forward to showing off his success to his father. He'd succeeded on his own. It was his diligence, his hard work, and his fortitude that had earned him a place in Tyson's urban army.

Shepherds
Yuliia Vereta

The wind carries radioactive dust
laying down on our best inventions.

The era of oil is now long forgotten,
the Internet of Things stores our dreams.

We graze stored electric current
on pastures of filled graphene panels.

Interspecies marriages got legalized,
the atmospheric dome is finally built.

The Silicon Age is coming to an end,
uranium lies at our feet like a silent beast.

The Spark
By Stephen C. Curro

Katrina grew up in a frigid world ruled by a tyrant. By day, she works as a mechanic. At night, she becomes the Ace, the King's personal assassin. She's not proud of her job, but she's accepted that it's the way things are. At least she has her boyfriend Dez and his little brother Uriah to light her life.

When Katrina is ordered to quash a rebel attack on the King's Command Center, she thinks it's just another job. But as she uncovers the plot, she is shocked to learn that Dez may be involved with the dissidents. Now Katrina must make an impossible choose—eliminate the one she loves, or defy the King she swore to serve.

The Spark is a sci-fi thriller about love, betrayal, and how the futures of others, even a whole civilization, can be determined through a single choice.

https://www.hiraethsffh.com/product-page/the-spark-by-stephen-c-curro

Red Moon Rising
By J Alan Erwine

J Alan Erwine takes you into a future environmental nightmare that is not only all too possible, but is in fact well on the way there. The air and seas are filthy with pollution and oil spills, the U.S. Government is an effete and toothless replica of its former self, and business decides which rules they will allow to be enforced. Corporations lie, people die.

Including Erik Singer's brother Jeromie, killed while seeking evidence against an oil company regarding their spills in the Gulf. After five years, Erik has had enough of wallowing in loss and self-pity. Emboldened by the words and visions of a Native American environmentalist, Erik is ready to act.

And he has colleagues. The reluctant mayor of Tampa. The daughter of the most egregious industrialist. And a tree-hugging terrorist. Can just four people make a difference?

https://www.hiraethsffh.com/product-page/red-moon-rising-by-j-alan-erwine

Sponged
James Dick

I think we might actually make it, Brie thought as she brought the escape pod to life. The few control panels that actually lit up spat sparks at her; a readout told her that one of the pod's engines had a cracked nozzle and wouldn't light, and she thought she smelled something metallic as the air scrubbers cycled. The escape pod was a death trap, but better to risk it than being melted by a giant space sponge.

"Forty seconds and we're out!" Brie shouted over her shoulder. Her call was answered by a *thump-CLACK* as a bright orange keg with the Starbräu logo on the side coasted through the escape pod hatch, hit the wall, and rebounded into a control panel, causing cracks to spiderweb across its LCD display. Ahmed poked his head through the hatch. "Two more kegs!" he said.

"Hurry!" Brie went back to her pre-flight checklist, which pretty much consisted of dumping as much reaction mass into the engines as they could handle.

While the nozzles chilled down, Brie accessed the *Starbräu Demeter*'s external cameras. The sponge's blue flesh had engulfed the long-range transceiver and the command centre. The parts of its flesh that made contact with the *Demeter*'s hull turned a lurid, almost beautiful shade of gold. No one could agree on what purpose the sponge's acidic secretions performed in their ecology—self-defence, chemical signalling, and a mating enzyme had all been suggested—but what they *could* agree on was that it was the most corrosive substance found in nature. Brie watched closely as the golden flesh brushed across a window. The window instantly blew out. The force of the air escaping from the decompressing module ripped a piece of the sponge's flesh away, sending it careening into the depths of the nebula. The sponge either didn't feel it or didn't care; it kept moving, dissolving any part of the ship it touched.

Another pair of kegs came through the hatch, as promised. One bounced off a wall and tumbled into the shuttle's stern compartments, the other flipped end-over-end and nudged Brie's jumpseat. "Watch it!" she called.

"Sorry," Ahmed grunted as he pulled himself through the hatch. He somersaulted into his jumpseat and buckled up.

Brie performed one final check of the shuttle's systems. "We're ready." She looked over her shoulder. "Where's Colin?"

Ahmed craned his neck to peer into the aft compartment. "He's not here?" He looked back at Brie, realization dawning on his face. "You don't think...?"

Brie groaned. "If that sponge doesn't kill him, I will." She started unbuckling herself.

A pair of legs dangled through the hatchway. "Pull me in, pull me in!" called a strangled voice.

Ahmed grabbed the legs and dragged Colin into the shuttle. Cradled in Colin's chest, completely unruffled by the klaxons, the shouting, or the bouncing about, was Edna, a golden Buff Orpington.

"You went back for the *chicken*?!" Brie hissed.

Colin gave her a helpless look. "I couldn't just leave her behind."

"Priorities, people," Ahmed said, pointing out the cockpit window.

Brie turned. A curtain of gold flesh wafted into view. The sponge had completely engulfed the *Demeter*. If even one leaf of its body touched the shuttle, they were all dead.

"Strap in," Brie snapped. "We're going." She grabbed the emergency release lever and waited.

"Be our luck if the hatch doesn't close," said Ahmed as he helped Colin with his seat harness.

"Think positive," Colin said.

Edna clucked.

The instant Brie heard the buckle of Colin's harness click home, she pulled the lever. The hatch slammed shut as the *Demeter* let the shuttle go, but not before Brie's ears popped and she felt the air surge toward the hatch just before it sealed. The deep spacers called that the "kiss of vacuum." Brie called it a close-kin lawsuit waiting to happen. Her readouts told her that they were clear of the ship, and she fired the dorsal thrusters to full power to put some distance between the shuttle and *Demeter* before opening up the main engines. When she did, she was crushed into her seat at two g's.

Brie saw the *Demeter* through one of the rear-facing cameras, almost entirely engulfed by the sponge. She saw the exact moment the hull collapsed: it was marked by a ballooning of the sponge's body, with pieces of its flesh flying off in every direction, as all the remaining gases aboard the *Demeter* escaped into the vacuum. The golden flesh of the sponge dimmed back to a cool blue, and the creature proceeded to investigate the decompressed corpse of the spacecraft.

Once the *Demeter* and its attacker dwindled to a faint grey-blue speck against the nebula, Brie cut the thrusters so her crew could catch their breath. "Everyone okay?" she asked, looking behind her.

Ahmed nodded stiffly.

Edna flapped her wings and clucked disapprovingly. "Shh," Colin cooed, running a finger over her beak. "It's all right, it's all right now."

Brie heaved a relieved sigh. "What about the booze?"

Ahmed unbuckled and floated to the back where the kegs had landed when the engines fired. "They're all intact. I think these kegs are the only reliable pieces of equipment Starbräu pays for."

Naturally, Brie thought. *Profit is all they care about.*

Ahmed looked back at her. "Speaking of reliable pieces of equipment... we should make sure the SCAB works. Cheap shuttle, after all."

Brie nodded and leaned over the arm of her jumpseat. She booted up the Superluminal Communication Array and Beacon and began scanning for a superluminal signal from *Starbräu Alpha Station*. The waveform travelling across her screen remained flat.

"C'mon, c'mon..." *Don't tell me we escaped just to die of asphyxiation...*

The waveform quivered.

"That's it." Brie zeroed in on the frequency. "*Alpha Station, Demeter S1. Alpha Station, Demeter S1,* are you receiving?"

A pause, and then a loud yawn echoed out of the speakers. "*Demeter S1, this is* Alpha. *How can we assist you on this fine, glorious, sunny day?*"

Brie looked at Ahmed. He was rolling his eyes. "Parker?" he mouthed.

Brie nodded. "Oh uh, you know," she said to the SCAB, "just wanted to call, see if the Pioneers beat the Kings, find out what's on the menu for dinner, and uh... oh yeah, our ship got sponged."

Another pause, followed by a heavy sigh. "*Great. What's that, third one this month?*"

* * *

Demeter's shuttle had no FTL drive, so Brie and her crew needed a pickup from *Alpha Station*. Parker informed Brie it would take a day to charge *Alpha Station*'s FTL drives. Nothing to do now but switch on the shuttle's beacon and wait. The adrenaline rush was over, and Brie saw her exhaustion reflected in Ahmed and Colin. (Edna, it seemed, remained unflappable.)

"I don't understand," said Ahmed. "We were well clear of the sponges' usual territory. We shouldn't have been attacked."

Brie shrugged. "No reckoning on the behaviour of wild animals."

"Hmm, not sure we can classify the sponges as 'animals,'" Colin said. He was feeding Edna food pellets he'd synthesized in the shuttle's nutrient mixer, but he remained attentive to the conversation. He spoke in a low, rapid tone, almost a mutter. "Animalia is a kingdom of multicellular, eukaryotic organisms. We're not sure if sponges possess either of those attributes, since no one's ever gotten a sample of one. There, there, who's a good chick?" Colin kissed Edna's head. She nuzzled his chin.

"Whatever they are," Brie continued, "I'm more pissed off about the fact that our early warning system didn't give us, you know, early warning when the sponge came calling."

Ahmed sighed and shook his head. "You *know* nothing on that ship had worked right in years."

"Okay, look, circuit boards shorting out? Fine. Nutrient mixers freezing? Sure. Air recyclers catching fire?"

Colin winced as if he'd been burned.

Brie instantly wished the words unsaid. "My point is," she hurried on, "I can handle all these things going wrong because I'm trained to handle them, but we all have to sleep sometime, and we can't have a sponge melting us while we're catching Z's. The early warning system should've woken us up sooner."

"One of us should always be on watch..." Ahmed started to say.

Brie ran right over him. "We're a crew of three!"

"Four," Colin said softly, scratching Edna's beak.

"We can't be expected to do a watch rotation *and* carry out a full collection schedule. The *only* reason we knew about the sponge was because Colin was awake taking care of his chic—taking care of Edna. That was blind luck!"

"Not really," Colin muttered. "I feed her on a regular basis."

"I hear what you're saying," Ahmed said, holding his hands up placatingly. "I just would've thought you'd know not to expect much from *Starbräu* at this point."

Brie ran her hands over her buzz cut hair and turned to the window. The galaxy's stars were veiled by a curtain of red-gold gas. "I did ten years on the Moon with the Northspace Group. You give your astronauts the best version of the best tools needed to do their job. You don't cheap out on them."

A brown hand with scarred fingers touched Brie's shoulder. "This isn't the Moon. This isn't Sol. This is the Kepler Frontier. We get new gear once, maybe twice a year.

Starbräu reuses everything. Out here, we make do with what we have."

"What we have," said Brie, without turning around, "isn't nearly enough."

Somewhere behind her, Edna clucked.

* * *

The night was long and cold. Ever the careful spacer, Brie turned down the heat a couple of degrees to save power. It wouldn't make a big difference in the long run, maybe a couple of minutes this or that way, if the unthinkable happened and *Alpha Station* never arrived, but just as the sponges were conditioned to protect their territory, Brie was conditioned to conserve her resources. *Starbräu* might not treat their tools properly, but Brie would.

During the artificial night Brie had created by dimming the lights, some long-trained instinct in her marrow woke her up. Her eyes snapped open, staring at her own reflection in a sleeping wall-mounted monitor. She kept perfectly still, floating in the middle of the cockpit while her ears parsed the quiet symphony of the space shuttle's vitals. There was a new sound, one that hadn't been there when Brie went to sleep. It was the ghostly, breathy sound of a man whispering in the dark.

As discreetly as she could, Brie turned her head and looked aft.

Edna was, from Brie's perspective, upside-down, roosting on a wall of the ship, her feet anchored in place by a weak adhesive. The chicken was fast asleep. Just past Edna, Ahmed slept swaddled in a full-body sleeping bag, breathing softly through his parted lips. Brie looked from Ahmed's sleeping bag to Colin's.

Colin was gone.

Brie squinted in the darkness and saw a shape huddled amongst the kegs in the aftermost compartment. She kicked off the pilot's seat and glided through the cabin toward the cargo hold. The shape resolved itself into Colin; he was curled up in the fetal position, head tucked between his arms, muttering rapidly to himself. His shoulders rose and fell with his short breaths.

"Colin," Brie whispered.

He didn't respond.

"Colin." Brie reached out and put a hand on Colin's shoulder. "Colin, it's okay. You're not there anymore."

"Feels like I'm always there," Colin whispered back, his words tumbling out like water from an overfull cup. "Always there."

"You're here, with us. We're safe. You're safe." Then, as an afterthought: "Edna's safe."

Colin chuckled. "I know you think it's weird, caring for animals more than people."

"Maybe I did, but not after today. There are still a few people I love." She massaged Colin between his shoulder blades.

"Appreciate it." Colin reached over his shoulder and placed his hand on hers.

"Did you come back here to be alone?"

Colin shook his ashy blonde locks. "Heard a clicking in my dreams, realized it was a loose air scrubber, woke up, came back here to find it." A pause. "Didn't mean to wake you. Didn't realize I was talking."

"It's good that you woke me. We can find the scrubber together."

"Okay." Colin pointed to a pallet of emergency food stuffs. "I think it's under there."

Brie didn't doubt Colin's ears for a second, and sure enough, there was a loose scrubber mounted inside a vent underneath the pallet. They worked together to lock it in place, then drifted forward to finish their sleep cycle. Colin wriggled into his sleeping bag and closed his eyes right away. Brie made sure he was secured and then headed for the cockpit. As she passed Ahmed, he opened his eyes. "Colin okay?" he asked.

Brie nodded. "Loose scrubber in the back."

Ahmed nodded and went back to sleep.

Brie made a cursory inspection of her ship's readouts before returning to sleep. There was nothing on the sensors, no annunciators demanding her attention. She felt wrung out. There was going to be an inquiry when they returned to *Alpha*, and her crew wasn't likely to get off easy.

Sleep now, worry then. Good advice from a good teacher back on Earth, but Brie had gotten so adept at worrying that she didn't have it in her to stop. Rather than take a sleeping bag, she went right back to hovering in the cockpit, listening to the sounds of her ship humming all around her.

* * *

The hearing room aboard *Alpha Station* was designed to make one feel surrounded. Seated at the centre of a semi-circular table, those summoned to appear before the administrators were made to feel beset on all sides. In Brie's case, that was exactly what was going on.

"Correct me if I'm wrong," said Tanith Broke, the station manager, "but this is now the third ship under your command you've lost."

Brie didn't even meet his gaze. She sat with her arms and legs crossed, head throbbing from a lack of sleep and an excess of bureaucracy. "That's right," she muttered.

"And it's the first ship with the advanced early warning system installed to detect sponges."

"Not much of a warning system..."

"I'm sorry, Harker, I didn't catch that."

Brie sighed. "You're correct."

"Okay, so, how is it that we're sitting here for the third time this month asking you the same questions about the same subjects?"

Brie fought the urge to roll her eyes. She knew she was being recorded, and she knew she was making a poor show already, but she was almost completely past the point of caring. "All I know," she said, "is that the early warning system didn't tell us a sponge was attacking. It was one of my crew who noticed the sponge sneaking up on us."

"Ah yes," said Broke. "Systems Specialist Colin Mercer. He's been on your crew for every one of these failures, hasn't he?"

For the first time, Brie looked at Tanith. "What's that supposed to mean?"

Tanith shrugged. "I'm simply establishing, for the record, that he was part of your crew."

"Yes, and I want to know why you want that on the record?"

The administrators all looked to Tanith, who stared Brie down. "Is it true that, on January 6th, 2390, Specialist Mercer was an employee of Aurora Space working aboard Whitson Orbital?"

White-hot rage kindled in Brie's chest. *How dare you...* "Again, why is this relevant?"

"And is it also true," Tanith pressed, "that on that particular date a fire broke out aboard the Whitson Orbital space station, killing six Aurora astronauts?"

"The incident's a matter of public record."

"What's *not* a matter of public record is Specialist Mercer's psychological profile following the incident." Tanith tapped on the tablet in front of him, summoning a psychiatrist's write-up on the wall screen for the whole committee to see. "I quote: 'Mercer possesses acute symptoms of post-traumatic stress disorder, including severe depression, anxiety, insomnia, and apprehension about taking on responsibility where human life is at stake. He describes recurring nightmares and thoughts of self-harm, and repeatedly states that he feels constant guilt over his inability to save his crewmates.' End quote." Tanith looked at Brie again. "Does this sound like someone who should be left alone to monitor the systems of a spacecraft? Frankly, I'm astounded you would choose to hire such an individual for your crew. I wouldn't let this man take charge of one of my goldfish, let alone one of my ships."

Murmurs rippled through the committee.

Brie never once looked at the psychiatrist's notes. She kept her eyes firmly on Tanith until she was ready to reply. When she did, it was two words, enunciated clearly for the record.

"Fuck. You."

Tanith's only visible reaction was a slight curling of the lips. "Care to expand?"

"Sure. Fuck you for trying to pin the loss of your precious booze on Colin." For the first time, Brie looked at the committee. "That report Tanith read you is from one month following the accident. One month! Nobody would be okay after only one month's recovery from a thing like that. But do you want to know what Colin's psych report says *eight* months after the accident? I can quote it from memory: 'Despite the devastating tragedy Mercer has experienced, he has repeatedly displayed positive coping mechanisms, a newfound respect for all living things, and an unparalleled attention to detail in his work as an astronaut. After lengthy evaluation, I believe he is ready and qualified to continue working in deep space.'" Brie let that sink in. A few of the committee were starting to look doubtfully at Tanith.

And Tanith felt it. He cleared his throat. "Let's not get sidetracked, here—"

"Colin was performing routine maintenance on a docked ship when the fire broke out," Brie continued. "The only reason he survived was because his commander sealed him off from the space station before the fire could reach him. He tried to override her lockouts to get back in and help them. He knew he'd probably burn to death before he could do anything, but if there was one shot in a million that he could make a difference, he was willing to take it."

"Harker," Tanith sighed, "the man keeps a *chicken* for a pet. On a *spacecraft*."

"And his pet is the reason I'm here right now. Your sensor array didn't work. The only reason I'm alive is because Colin looked out a window while taking care of Edna." Brie stood up. "You wanna drop the axe of 'human error' on somebody, maybe it should be on the ones who sent us into the nebula with bad gear."

* * *

Brie followed the slowly curving habitat ring to *Alpha Station*'s built-in bar. Sweeping windows gave a spectacular view of the coral-coloured clouds of the nebula. The clouds turned lazy circles as the hab ring rotated.

Brie found Ahmed, Colin, and Edna sitting at a table in the corner, far away from the other company employees. Getting sponged was nothing to be ashamed of. Getting sponged three times in a month, well...

"'Grounded without pay due to a severe lack of judgment and the questionable mental state of your crew,'" Brie said, quoting from the tablet in her hand. She spun a chair around and straddled it, tossing the tablet onto the table for her crewmates to read.

Ahmed looked over the rim of his scotch glass at the screen. "Ah. Well, that was to be expected." From the way he slurred his vowels, Brie guessed he was a few cups deep already.

"It's bullshit, is what it is," said Brie.

Colin fed Edna some synthetic seeds. "Hmm... where does that leave us?"

"Stranded on this station with our dwindling savings," Brie replied. "They've also strapped us with a fine for items lost when the *Demeter* broke up. Because of that, we're deemed a flight risk, so we can't board a transport out."

"Have to admit," said Colin, his lips turning downward, "as far as reprimands from the company go, holding us prisoner is new." He didn't seem as perturbed as Brie would've expected.

Ahmed crossed his arms and frowned at the glass sitting in front of him, trying to find something hidden in its depths.

"Whatcha thinking?" Brie asked.

"That this," said Ahmed, looking at her, "this grounding, it isn't just about punishment. Think about it: they might not be paying us, but they're still giving us room and board. If they really wanted to punish us, they'd fire us and ship us out on the earliest transport. This doesn't feel like punishment to me."

Brie shrugged. "What does it feel like?"

Ahmed drummed his fingers on his elbow. "A holding pattern."

Colin's eyes locked onto something past Brie's shoulder and widened. "Tanith."

Brie rotated in her seat.

Tanith had indeed stepped into the bar. He was carrying two bottles of whiskey; not the kind served in the bar, but the kind served only on the executive level. Whiskey from Earth. He came straight over to the grounded crew's table wearing a demure expression. "That seat taken?" he asked, nodding to the single unoccupied chair.

Brie was tempted to tell Colin to set Edna down in the empty chair so she could have a reason to turn Tanith away, but Colin would never use Edna like that, so there was no point. Brie gestured for Tanith to take it, which he did.

Tanith set the bottles on the table and clasped his hands. "There was no way the committee was going to accept responsibility for the countermeasure failure."

"What a shock," Brie said dryly, eyeing the amber liquid before her.

"And for what it's worth..." Tanith glanced at Colin. "I'm sorry I used Mr. Mercer's record as ammunition."

Colin raised an eyebrow and looked at Brie. "The fire?" he asked.

Brie nodded.

"Ah." Colin went back to feeding Edna.

"Truth be told," Tanith continued, "I actually consider Mercer quite—"

"What do you want?" Brie interrupted, finally looking at Tanith.

Tanith opened his hands. "To make you an offer."

"This should be good," Ahmed grumbled.

Tanith ignored him. "The loss of your ship was the straw that broke the camel's back. We were going to ground the next crew that got sponged, and it's just your bad luck that it was you."

Brie stared at Tanith. "You... what?"

"Let me finish," he said. He reached into his pocket, took out a tablet, and placed it on the table. The screen displayed a graph with two lines: one red, one blue, both rising in tandem. "The blue line represents volume of alcohol collected from the nebula. The red one represents sponge attacks. I don't think I need to tell you what this means."

It took a moment for Brie to grasp the magnitude of what Tanith was showing her.

Everyone thought that sponge attacks were a territorial response: the deeper a ship went into the nebula, the higher the chances of being attacked. Of course, there was a payoff for going deeper: that's where the denser alcohol clouds lay. But this graph suggested that the attacks had nothing to do with territoriality, that the sponges were in fact going after ships with high volumes of alcohol in their holds.

"The exobiology commission hasn't seen this, have they?" Brie asked.

"No," said Tanith, taking the tablet back, "and if you breathe a word of this on the net, we'll deny it. The company's permit to mine the nebula is contingent on the theory that the sponges are territorial. If the commission were to learn that mining the nebula was *inherently* dangerous, instead of *incidentally*—"

"They'd revoke your permit," said Brie, "and you'd face lawsuits from every spacer who ever worked this nebula for you, because you lied to them. You lied to us."

"We didn't lie," Tanith replied tactically. "We simply operated on a different theory of the sponges' behaviour. A theory that held water, until now."

"What's changed?" Colin asked with detached curiosity.

"Over the last year, we've gotten an increasing number of queries from the exobiology commission. They want to know why the rate of sponge attacks is going up, even though we aren't delving that deep into the nebula. The theory of territoriality is starting to buckle. At the next hearing, we have to release this graph. We don't want to do it without a countermeasure." At an incredulous look from Brie's crew, he hastily added, "A *real* countermeasure."

"So, what do you need us for?" Brie asked.

"Simple. We want you to find out why the sponges attack ships with higher volumes of alcohol."

All three of the crew scoffed. Edna clucked disapprovingly.

"Ten years of mining," Ahmed said, "and you only *now* decide to answer that question?"

Tanith shrugged. "Bureaucracy."

"How exactly do you expect us to figure that out?" Brie asked.

Tanith opened a new window on the tablet. "After attacking a laden ship, sponges always retreat to the centre of the nebula." He slid the tablet toward them. This time, the image was a starburst pattern, showing the trajectories of sponges leading deep into the heart of the cloud. "Every time, without fail. And when we perform an analysis of a ship's wreckage, all alcohol is missing. The sponges must be taking it with them. The question is where, and why."

Brie looked at the chart, then at Tanith. "And you expect us to figure this out for you... why?"

"We'll restore you to flight status and expunge your record. We'll also triple your hazard pay for the mission. Of course, if you'd like to find employment elsewhere, you'll have glowing commendations to take with you."

"We'd need a ship for this mission," Colin observed.

"We'll outfit you with a Prospector. Top of the line."

"What's to stop us from getting in the ship and leaving?" Ahmed asked.

"The ship will have a safeguard built in," Tanith explained with a sneer. "A sensor will keep track of particle density in the cloud. If it drops below a certain threshold, the ship will stop dead in its tracks, and you'll have to turn back."

"Why not just send an unmanned probe and save all this hassle?" Brie asked.

"The particle density deeper in the cloud blocks all communication. We'd have no way to control the probe or receive telemetry. This really is the only way." He looked straight at Brie. "We're not bullshitting you," he said. "We want our crews to be safe as much as you do. If we know why the sponges do what they do, that might give us a chance to save ships, maybe even save lives."

Brie scrutinized Tanith. "You willing to put all this in writing?"

"Absolutely," Tanith said without hesitation.

Brie looked to her crewmates. "What do you say?"

"A chance to learn about strange life forms?" said Colin. "Kinda why I got into space to begin with."

Brie smiled and turned to Ahmed.

"If it stops another crew from getting sponged," he said, "I'm in."

Brie looked at Tanith. "Okay, you've got your crew."

Tanith grinned. Then he looked at Edna. "Any chance you'd leave the chicken—"

"Edna goes," Colin said, meeting Tanith's gaze squarely. "Non-negotiable."

* * *

Tanith wasn't kidding about giving them a state-of-the-art ship. *Prospector 14* was a small ship, only a little bit bigger than the escape shuttle they'd used to evacuate from the *Demeter*. Lean and fast.

Brie and Ahmed sat in the cockpit, completing the last of their pre-flight checks, while Edna did her best to distract them. She clucked and cawed, but Brie could do nothing for the chicken. Colin was outside, performing his exterior walkabout ("walkabout" being the antiquated word for it; he was floating around the exterior of the ship in a spacesuit).

Every now and again, when Edna complained, Brie shot the bird a scathing look. *You used to be a dinosaur,* she thought. Now *look at you.*

Edna fixed one of her beady eyes at Brie, quite cannily.

"She is kind of adorable," Ahmed said of the chicken.

"Don't you start..." Brie warned.

The door to the cockpit slid open and Colin entered, sans his EVA kit. "Okay, all done."

Brie nodded. "Take a seat, we're just about ready."

Colin obeyed, strapping himself into the mission specialist's chair. "You know, if this works," he said, "I think you owe Edna *two* apologies."

Brie rolled her eyes. "Let's not get ahead of ourselves." She opened the channel to the station. "Alpha tower, *P-14*, we're showing greens across the board."

The tower controller replied, *"Tower copies. Say the word, and we'll cut you loose."*

"Word is said. Send it."

There was an almighty clang, and Brie and her crew went into freefall as the *Prospector* hurtled out into space, carried by the centrifugal force imparted by Alpha Station's rotation. Brie took a moment to savour the feeling of weightlessness before opening up the throttle. "Thank you, Alpha. We're free and clear."

There was a crunch followed by wet mastication over the mic. *"Mmm... copy, P-14, come home safe."*

Brie smirked. "Will do." She glanced at the disk of Alpha in the ventral camera feed. The station rapidly shrank to the size of a coin, then vanished amidst the stars.

Before them loomed the particle clouds.

A dying ship wasn't hard to track. It left behind all manner of traces: escaped gases, hot metal, and hard radiation. Brie had no trouble charting a course back to the region where the *Demeter* had been attacked. Most of the wreckage was still there. Even at a distance of several kilometres, Brie could tell the alcohol collectors had been ruptured.

Ahmed threw a holographic display of the sponge's trajectory onto the cockpit glass. The green line of the sponge's propulsive gases described a curve from the *Demeter* to the heart of the nebula.

Brie was struck by the realization of just how strange this nebula was. Most nebulae were more tenuous than the thinnest wisp of cloud. From a thousand light year distance, they seemed like vast reefs teeming with baby stars, but once you plunged into their depths, the sky only looked a little different than when you were outside. Maybe there'd be a slight discolouration of the space between stars, but that was all. Space inside a nebula was not much different than space outside it.

But this place was different. Here, the gases clotted together, thicker than any fog bank, utterly obscuring the interior of the nebula behind curtains of orange opaqueness. Even among the alcohol-rich nebulae that dotted the Milky Way galaxy, the *Starbräu* Motherlode was an aberration. Something in Brie's mind rebelled against the notion of falling blindly through those clouds. She'd never been given to thalassophobia, but she got a small taste of it peering down into those luminous, murky depths.

"You know, I just thought of something?" she said aloud. "On a planet orbiting a star in any nebula in the galaxy, you could still look up and see the Milky Way. But in there..." she nodded toward the clouds. "You can't. We can't see in, and no one can see out. A civilization could evolve, live, and die, never realizing they were part of a greater cosmos."

The cockpit was silent for some time following her statement. Even Edna seemed like she needed a moment to take in the thought.

Suddenly, Colin said, "Actually, you're wrong."

Brie craned her head around. "Come again?"

Colin flashed her a bashful smile. "The sponges. Any civilization inside the nebula would look up, see the sponges, and watch as they passed through the clouds in the sky. The people would naturally assume the sponges go *somewhere*. They'd spend thousands of years dreaming about following the creatures, and when they finally do, they'll find us waiting."

"They'll find *Starbräu* waiting," Ahmed corrected. "And *Starbräu* would find a way to exploit them, I'm sure."

"Maybe," said Colin. "But right now, whoever is in there is hidden. The inside of that cloud is probably the safest place in the galaxy. The gases slow down deadly cosmic rays, the sponges discourage intruders, and radio signals can't get out." He paused, and then added, "This cloud is a cosmic womb."

Another long silence passed.

Brie opened the throttle slowly. "Best get moving."

They passed into the clouds, keeping careful watch for the telltale vacuoles caused by the passage of sponges. No ship had ventured this deep into the nebula in three years, and they were about to pass the point which no ship had ever penetrated.

"Hundred-thousand kilometres to the barrier," Ahmed said. "Fifty-thousand. Crossing... now."

The colour of the clouds abruptly changed. They went from orange-pink to green-blue.

"Uh..." Brie said. "Okay, I'm pretty sure this is physically impossible."

"It's almost as if the nebula is organized," said Colin. "I'm watching the spectrographs now. The alcohol content in the clouds just plummeted. I'm seeing heavier elements everywhere, especially noble gases."

"What the hell is this place..." Brie muttered, watching as the texture of the clouds became smoother, less fluffy, almost like watercolours.

"Brie," said Ahmed, "we just crossed a vacuole. A big one. A sponge passed through here, maybe an hour ago."

"I have an idea," said Colin. "I'm going to expel some helium over the skin of the ship. Should wash us clean of alcohol particles."

Brie nodded. "So the sponges will lose interest in us."

"Spectrographs are going crazy," said Ahmed. "Heavy elements are spiking. LIDAR is blind."

"Reducing speed—whoa!" Brie brought the ship to a full stop. Her jaw fell open in awe. Her crewmates might've uttered expletives; if they did, she didn't hear it.

They'd broken through into some kind of hollow space, millions of kilometres in diameter. At the centre of it, perhaps three-hundred thousand kilometres end-to-end, was a structure. Not artificial; organic. It was blue, and had the same texture as the sponges, only rougher, and the sponges themselves were moving over its surface.

"Guys," Brie said, "what are we looking at?"

"Working," Colin said, as if the most magnificent sight in the galaxy was just another math problem. "Okay, if I'm reading this right, the structure is made of a combination of crystallized alcohol, heavy elements, and sponge tissue."

Ahmed broke out of his stupor and began studying the thing as well. "Sensors have clear lines of sight. They're tracking approximately three-thousand sponges of various sizes moving over the surface of the structure... including the one that attacked us."

"Show me," Brie ordered.

A holo-window appeared on the glass of the cockpit, zoomed in on one of the sponges. It looked to be depositing roughly shaped objects onto the structure, building it out, expanding it.

"It almost looks like... a coral reef," Brie mused.

"That may not be far from the truth," said Colin. "It's alive, or at least contains massive quantities of organic matter, but it's not mobile in the way that the sponges are. There's none of the same propulsive matter being outgassed."

"And based on the small size of some of those sponges," Ahmed added, "I think it's pretty clear this is a nursery as well."

Brie shook her head in disbelief. "A living reef... ten times larger than the diameter of the Earth... suspended in the centre of a particle cloud." She shut her eyes and opened them. The reef was still there. "And all we wanted to do was mine this place for booze, as a gimmick."

Brie felt a hand on her shoulder. Colin had untethered himself from his seat and floated over to her, with Edna under one arm. "The exobiology commission has to know," he said. "This goes beyond any corporate concern. This," he nodded toward the reef, filling the cockpit window despite being hundreds of thousands of kilometres distant. "This is what I went into space to see."

"Me too," said Ahmed. There was a tremor in the man's voice. Brie turned around and saw his lower lip quivering.

Brie had never thought of herself as an altruist or a true explorer. She'd gone into space to make a living. But she could not look at that vast reef and be unmoved.

She made a decision. "I guess," she said slowly, "we're about to find out if that little countermeasure of yours worked, Colin."

Colin smiled.

Edna clucked.

Brie looked one last time at the reef. She had no idea when she might see it again, if ever, and she wanted to fix this sight in her mind. She zoomed in on the sponge that had destroyed her ship. The creature was still torn and wounded, but as she watched, it stretched out along a curved, fluted whelk of the reef and pressed its body flat against the surface. A beautiful interplay of colour and motion ensued, wherein the sponge seemed to surrender pieces of itself to the reef, and regenerated its damaged tissues in turn.

"It's depositing the alcohol it took from us," Brie said, "and receiving matter to rebuild its body."

"Seems like it," said Colin.

Brie sighed. "All right, boys and ornithoids, buckle up. It's quitting time."

* * *

Tanith Broke never took a gamble he wasn't certain would pay off.

The Chairman, wizened old lich that he was, had doubted that the crew of the *Demeter* would take the deal to probe the unexplored heart of the particle cloud. Tanith had taken no small amount of satisfaction when Harker's team had acceded. The look on the Chairman's face alone was worth it.

Now, the ancient whitehead sat in a chair in the executive suite, sipping scotch that was almost as old as he was, and took in the view through the panoramic window. Tanith sat across from him, nursing a gin and tonic.

"Shouldn't they be back by now?" the Chairman asked in his raspy tenor.

Tanith shrugged. "Depends on what they found. No one knows anything about the sponges. Not really, anyway."

The old man scowled. "A fact I've come to regret..."

"We all have," said Tanith. He raised his glass. "Don't sweat it, sir. We'll have our answers."

Right on cue, a chime sounded in the lounge. *"Mr. Broke,"* said Goran, the flight controller of the day, over the intercom. *"We have a contact emerging from the nebula. It's P-14."*

"Ah, wonderful," said Tanith, setting his glass on a low crystal coffee table and rising from his chair. "Open comms, if you please, and make sure we're writing everything to hard drive." Tanith smiled at the Chairman. "Have to keep detailed records."

The old lich swirled the ice in his glass, but otherwise didn't react.

Brie Harker's voice echoed in the lounge, causing the nearby execs to lower their drinks and listen in. *"Alpha, P-14. Am I speaking with Tanith?"*

"You are, Harker," said Tanith. "Go ahead."

There was a pause. *"Tanith, you are a piece of shit, and I'm glad I don't have to work for you anymore."*

A gasp rippled throughout the lounge.

The Chairman cocked an eyebrow.

Tanith's eyebrows hit the roof. "Excuse me—"

"Sir!" Goran interrupted. *"The* Prospector, *she's not slowing down. She's accelerating out of the nebula!"*

They could all see it: a tiny star, trailing plasma, rocketing toward the void.

"Brie," Tanith sighed, "don't be stupid. You know there's a—"

"Lockout on the controls?" A new voice this time: Colin Mercer's. *"Yeah, funny thing about that. You had the lockout function based on particle density. As long as the sensor detects a certain particle count outside the ship, we can't leave the nebula."*

"What's your point, Mercer?" Tanith asked.

"Sir, they're reaching the nebula boundary..." Goran said.

"My point," said Mercer, "is that, although I'm not sure what the particle density of the nebula is, but I'm pretty sure a chicken's egg yolk exceeds it by an order of magnitude. So, I smeared one over the sensor."

There was a pause, and laughter rippled throughout the lounge. Even the Chairman was cracking a smile.

Tanith's cheeks burned.

That damned chicken of Mercer's clucked over the speakers. "Yes, Edna," Mercer cooed, "you could definitely say he's got egg on his face."

"Might as well accept my resignation, while we're at it," said a third voice, Ahmed Dawud. "I wish I could say it was a pleasure, sir, but we both know that would be a lie."

"*Prospector* has cleared nebula boundary!" Goran shouted. "FTL drives cycling. The lockout failed, sir!"

"I can see that, thank you, Goran," Tanith muttered. He thought fast. There had to be a way to salvage this. After all, they'd only be out a single ship—

"Sir," said Goran, "we're getting a data packet from the... oh my..."

Tanith's tablet chimed, as did the tablets of every exec in the lounge... including the Chairman. Tanith retrieved his and looked at the information streaming in.

"By now," said Harker, "you're probably seeing pictures of what we found at the heart of the cloud. Naturally, we'll be showing this to the exobiology commission upon our return to Earth. You should expect to hear from them in a week or so. Anyway, see you around!"

Tanith ran to the window and pounded on it. "Brie, dammit, you turn that ship around—"

Too late. Brie and her crew vanished in a flash of light, taking a trillion-dollar spacecraft and the death warrant of *Starbräu* with them.

Tanith suddenly felt cold, very cold indeed. A towering presence rose up behind him, and he turned to see the Chairman on his feet, shooting his cuffs.

"Mr. Broke," the Chairman whispered, "I wonder if I might see you in my office in, say, five minutes."

A wave of nausea overcame Tanith, and he rushed to a nearby trash chute to vomit.

"Hmm..." the Chairman muttered, turning on his heel. "Perhaps ten would suffice."

A Stop At Willoughby Exposes The Horror Possible In The Male Role and in Foolish Nostalgia
Denise Noe

The brainchild of writer Rod Serling, the original *Twilight Zone* was a half-hour anthology series that aired 1959 to 1964. It won fame for thriller, science fiction, fantasy, and horror stories. Episodes opened with Serling narrating: "There is a fifth dimension beyond that which is known to man. It is a dimension as vast as space and as timeless as infinity. It is the middle ground between light and shadow, between science and superstition, and it lies between the pit of man's fears and the summit of his knowledge. This is the dimension of imagination. It is an area which we call *The Twilight Zone*."

One of *TZ*'s most effective episodes was "A Stop At Willoughby" that first aired May 6, 1960. It opens in a boardroom. At the head of the table is Mr. Misrell (Howard Smith). The camera focuses on anxious looking Gart Williams (James Daly).

Speaking to Gart, Misrell observes, "We're still waiting for your Mr. Ross."

Gart goes to a phone where he calls someone and asks questions about Ross. After the call, Gart grimaces. There is a knock at the door. Gart answers. Someone hands him a letter. Gart says, "This is a communication from Jake Ross. . . . He's resigned, moving to another agency -- and taking the automobile account with him."

Misrell explodes, "Your pet project backfired!. . . This is a push-push-push business!"

"Pushed" passed his limits, Gart screams, "Fat boy, why don't you shut your mouth!" Gart flees the room, entering a secretarial pool.

A worker asks if Gart wants anything. "A razor and a chart of the human anatomy showing where the arteries are," he replies, bitterly joking about suicide. He goes into his personal office.

Serling states: "This is Gart Williams, age thirty-eight, a man protected by a suit of armor, all held together by one bolt. Just a moment ago, someone removed the bolt, and Mr. Williams' protection fell away from him and left him a naked target. He's been cannonaded this afternoon by all the enemies of his life. His insecurity had shelled him, his sensitivity has straddled him with humiliation, his deep-rooted disquiet about his own worth has zeroed in on him, landed on target, and blown him apart. Mr. Gart Williams, ad agency exec who, in just a moment, will move into *The Twilight Zone* in a desperate search for survival."

Excellent acting helps make the forgoing scene powerful. Daly is sympathetic as the stressed-out executive; Smith plays the overbearing boss perfectly. The name "Misrell" suggests "misery."

The next scene finds Gart on a commuter train. The middle-aged conductor (Jason Wingreen), asks Gart how he is. Gart fibs, "In the absolute pink." The two chat about the winter weather; the audience sees snow through the window.

Misrell's "push push push" plays through Gart's mind. Gart blurts, "That's enough!" Gart is embarrassed to realize he has said it aloud.

Gart takes a nap. Awakening, he is puzzled to see an oddly old-fashioned lamp on the ceiling. An elderly conductor (James Maloney) calls out, "Willoughby!" At the time he makes this call, the train is deserted except for the conductor and Gart.

Looking out the window, Gart sees a scene bathed in sunshine: people wear late 19th Century clothing, a dog barks, two boys (Billy Booth and Butch Hengen) walk holding fishing poles, and carriage driver (Max Slaten) waves at Gart.

Gart asks the conductor, "Where is Willoughby?"

"That's Willoughby right outside," the conductor

answers.

Gart says he cannot understand the sunshine in November. The conductor says it is "July 1888." Gart again inquires about Willoughby and the conductor explains, "It's really a lovely little village – peaceful, restful, where a man can slow down to a walk and live his life full measure."

Gart awakens a second time. He sees the original conductor who is calling, "Westport Saugatuck!"

Baffled, Gart asks, "You ever hear of a town called Willoughby?"

The conductor states, "There's no Willoughby on this line."

The next scene takes place in an upper-middle class home. Gart's wife Janie (Patricia Donahue) watches her husband put ice cubes into a drink and sarcastically inquires, "What are your plans for this evening? To get quietly plastered and then sing old college songs?" The wife of a man in the boardroom informed Janie of the day's events. Janie asks, "Did you wreck a career this afternoon? Did you throw away a job?"

Gart answers that Misrell "has found it in that great oversized heart of his to forgive" and speculates that it might be for fear that Gart would take business with him if he worked for another company. Gart continues, "I'm tired, Janie. I'm tired and I'm sick."

"You're on the right ward," she remarks. "We specialize in people who are sick – and tired too, Gart. I'm tired of a husband who lives in a kind of permanent self-pity with a heart bleeding sensitivity that he unfurls like a flag whenever he decides the competition is a little too rough for him."

Gart protests, "Some people aren't built for competition." He calls himself a "very un-competitive, rather dull, quite uninspired, average type guy – with a wife who has an appetite."

"And where would you be if it weren't for my appetite?" she asks.

He answers, "I know where I'd like to be. . . A place called Willoughby – a little town I manufactured in a dream." Janie asks him to describe the dream. Gart appears transported with joy as he recalls, "It was summer, very warm, kids were barefooted – one of them had a fishing pole. It all looked like a Currier and Ives painting: a bandstand, bicycles, wagons. I've never seen such serenity. It was the way people must have lived a hundred years ago."

Janie says, "You know what the trouble with you is, Gart? You were just born too late -- because you're the kind of guy who could be satisfied with a summer afternoon or an ice wagon being drawn by a horse. So it's my mistake, pal, my error, my miserable tragic error to get married to a man whose big dream in life is to be Huckleberry Finn!" She storms upstairs.

Commenting on this scene, Todd VanDerWerff claims the scene "doesn't entirely work" because "it's clear that we're meant to see her as another villainous person holding Gart down." Yet VanDerWerff sympathizes with her "as a woman who has had enough of her husband's fantasies and his refusal to take responsibility for his own happiness in the life he already has. . . . When she dismisses his fantasies as being out of *Huckleberry Finn*, it's a great line because there is truth to it."

My take is that regardless of how we are "meant" to see Janie, the scene works *because* of – not despite – her ambiguities.

Alone, Gart mulls the 1888 conductor's description of Willoughby as "a place where a man can live his life full measure."

The next scene shows Gart back on the train. Wingreen-as-conductor tells Gart, "I looked up Willoughby on every old time table I could find" but saw "no such place." Gart concludes it was just "a dream."

Then Gart falls asleep – and is awakened by Maloney-as-conductor calling "Willoughby!" Gart looks out at the tranquil scene and hears a band playing. Then he awakens again in the 1960 train. Quietly he vows, "Next time I'm going to get off at Willoughby."

We see Gart in his office. The receiver is off the phone and lying on the desk. We hear Misrell exclaiming,

"What we need here, Williams, is a show with zaz, an entertainer with moxie!" Gart repeats a desultory "I understand" between Misrell's "push-push-push" exhortations. Misrell asserts, "Tomorrow morning I want at least a preliminary idea for the show. . . . Just a rough format with a few details as to how we integrate the commercials within the body of the show." When Gart promises to "do the best I can," Misrell says, "Do more than you can! . . . Push push push!" That call ends but another phone – there are two phones on Gart's desk – rings. Gart attempts to placate person on that call when the other phone rings. Holding a phone receiver at each ear, he becomes increasingly flustereds. Office worker Helen (Mavis Neal) comes in the room and says, "Mr. Misrell would like to see you." Gart does not respond and Helen repeats, "Mr. Misrell would like to see you!"

Gart drops the phones and rushes into a bathroom. In the mirror over the sink, Gart sees disembodied Misrell faces repeating "Push push push!" Gart slams the mirror with his hand.

Gart returns to his office and phones Janie. He says, "I'm coming home. Will you stay there? No, honey. Listen, please, I've had it, understand? I've had it. I can't take this another day, not another hour." We hear a cold *click* of the phone. His wife has refused him comfort in his time of need.

Back on the train, the conductor played by Wingreen calls, "Stamford!" Gart falls asleep. He awakens to Maloney calling, "Willoughby!"

Gart looks outside the window and sees people walking around in 19th Century garments. A band plays a lively, old-fashioned tune. The smiling conductor points to the outside of the train. Gart stands, holding his briefcase. He looks at the briefcase and then leaves it behind on the seat. The conductor leads Gart off the train. Two boys with fishing poles and fishes greet Gart. "Hi, Mr. Williams!" one exclaims.

"Catch some big ones today, huh?" Gart asks. "I think tomorrow I'll join you."

As Gart walks further into Willoughby, the carriage

driver says, "Hi ya, Mr. Williams. Welcome."

"Thank you," Gart says. "I'm glad to be here." He shows no puzzlement at being recognized by Willoughby residents.

Gart continues walking. The camera turns to focus on the conductor, who smiles approvingly. Then both the view of the conductor and audience go to the swinging of a clock's pendulum.

The scene darkens – literally -- and we see a lantern swinging. The man with the lantern approaches the conductor played by Wingreen and asks, "Just jumped off the train, did he?"

Wingreen nods. "Shouted something about Willoughby, then ran out to the platform and that is the last I saw of him," he recounts. "Doctor says he must have died instantly. They're going to take him into town for an autopsy. Funeral parlor there sent the ambulance."

That ambulance is from "Willoughby & Son Funeral Home."

The episode ends with Serling saying: "Willoughby? Maybe it's wishful thinking nestled in a hidden part of a man's mind or maybe it's the last stop in the vast design of things. Or perhaps for a man like Mr. Gart Williams who climbed in a world that went by too fast, it's a place around the bend where he could jump off. Willoughby? Whatever it is, it comes with sunlight and serenity and is a part of *The Twilight Zone*."

The episode's ending is puzzling. Writers often describe Gart's death as a suicide, an interpretation recalling his sardonic jest about wanting a razor and chart of arteries. I think they are wrong. Gart's death was an accident. He wanted to "live his life full measure." However, he allowed his *wish* for Willoughby to become *belief* in Willoughby. Believing an illusion killed him.

And what of Willoughby & Son Funeral Home? Jordan Prejean derides it as "nonsensical," asserting it "makes no sense at all other than to serve as a sly, albeit confusing, wink to the viewer."

I believe we are meant to surmise that Gart may have encountered the Willoughby & Son Funeral Home. At some level, Gart knows it is dangerous to attempt to live in a fantasy world, so his subconscious mind named the fantasized village after a business dedicated to the dead.

Ultimately, much of what makes "A Stop At Willoughby" haunting is that it both critiques the grim possibilities inherent in the traditional male role and warns against romanticizing the past.

There certainly have been areas in which women have been – and still are – unfairly discriminated against. Laws forbidding discrimination against women in the workplace should be rigorously enforced. However, it remains true that women have always had, and to a large extent still have, an "out" from the workplace in the form of full-time homemaking.

It does not diminish the legitimacy of women's gender-specific grievances to recognize that men have special problems. One men's problem is that, generally speaking, they have no "out" from the paid labor market. Today there are more "stay-at-home-dads" and househusbands than in 1960 but they remain far fewer in number than stay-at-home-moms and housewives. It is likely women are less apt to be willing to support a dependent husband than vice versa.

Some people of both sexes are not built for the competition of the labor market – but females have an alternative. In Letty Cotton Pogrebin's first book, *How To Make It In A Man's World*, a chapter is entitled "If You Can't Stand The Heat, Get Back To The Kitchen." Pogrebin makes it clear that *some* women do not belong in the workforce and are better off as full-time homemakers. However, few men even today have this option; fewer still had it in 1960. Thus, like many men, Gart has a sense of being imprisoned by his job. The briefcase to Gart does not symbolize power but oppression.

Romanticizing past time periods is a common human tendency but one that is inherently unrealistic. People living through the 1880s, commonly called "The Gilded Age," would probably have scoffed at Gart's perception that their period was a peaceful idyll. The decade saw the assassination of Russia's Czar Nicholas II with pogroms because Jews were blamed for it. It saw the assassination of America's President James Garfield, the banditry of Billy the Kid and Jesse James, and the rampage of England's Jack the Ripper.

It is likely that people living in any period have always and will always view "these days" as days of special stress. "These days" were probably seen that way by pre-historical cave dwellers and will be seen that way when humans have settled on other planets.

Even though romanticizing past eras is unrealistic, it has benefits by inspiring artistic endeavors and enjoyable role-playing. However, it is also dangerous. There is no time travel in reality and no utopia. Thus, the friendly, even avuncular 1880s train conductor beckoning Gart to the village where he can "live his life full measure" is actually beckoning him to his doom. The conductor could be seen allegorically as a devil or demon. But perhaps more simply, he represents the destructiveness inherent in blurring the line between fantasy and reality.

"A Stop At Willoughby" works as entertainment because it is a well-crafted show. It haunts long after being viewed because it explores deep truths.

Bibliography

"A Stop At Willoughby."
https://www.youtube.com/watch?v=v50bfgBAX4o

"A Stop At Willoughby."
http://www.imdb.com/title/tt0734550/

"A Stop At Willoughby" script.
http://www.springfieldspringfield.co.uk/view_episode_scripts.php?tv-show=the-twilight-zone-1959&episode=s01e30

"Exploring the Twilight Zone #30: A Stop At Willoughby."
https://filmschoolrejects.com/exploring-the-twilight-zone-30-a-stop-at-willoughby-aeda25b2d969#.ul1mflqad

"Original *Twilight Zone* Episode List."

http://www.twilightzoneepisodesguide.com/

Prejean, Jordan. "A Stop At Willoughby." The Twilight Zone Vortex. May 4, 2012. http://twilightzonevortex.blogspot.com/2012/05/stop-at-willoughby.html

"Timeline from 1880 to 1890." http://history1800s.about.com/od/timelines/a/1880-1890-timeline.htm

VanDerWerff, Todd. "*The Twilight Zone*: 'Nightmare As A Child'/'A Stop At Willoughby." *The Twilight Zone. TV Club.* Jan. 7, 2012. http://www.avclub.com/tvclub/the-twilight-zone-nightmare-as-a-childa-stop-at-wi-67228

Breathing Real Air
Casey Richards-Bradt

Bruna felt qualified for a job that no longer existed. She was eighteen and only had six months at the Juneau, Alaska Super Target on her resume. She had only kept the job because she doubted her managers knew she worked there. She didn't even remember the name of the woman who had welcomed her on her first day. She would silently clock in from her watch and fold clothes for six hours without a manager's hello, direction, or correction. After orientation, she was trusted by the company to fold clothes all on her own. This meant taking the shirt lumps the automated machines attempted to fold and refolding them. The overlords at the Juneau Super Target had eyes from all angles that they could implement if need be. But the store was so vast and blank on weekdays that Bruna imagined the cameras as bored; imagined her quasi-imaginary managers as uncaring. She began leaving her station for hours during her shifts. She felt there were only so many times she could mimic a simple task for a rudimentary machine. She'd take four-hour-long breaks, walking half-marathons and eavesdropping on customers in the cafe. One time she took a nap in one of the display beds in the bedding aisle and woke up with eyes high on dreams, smelling like fresh linen.

One morning in November, it rained after a freak snowstorm, and Bruna showed up to the fluorescent warehouse to find it unlocked, but empty. Not a single other employee was in the store or the parking lot. Not even the security guard. Not a limb. She was the only one who had shown up for work, but the doors slid open for her. Inside the windows, she could see the machines raising and lowering their arms forever, building a tower of acid-wash jeans. She sat befuddled on a red orb, not knowing whether to call her boss or her mother. But she didn't know what hypothetical boss' name to search for in her contacts. She would need a ride home from her mom, but her mom would be pissed if she had to turn the car around now. She'd yell about gas prices.

Bruna clocked into work on her watch for the last time and started walking away from the store, befuddled. She took the last three pieces of gum out of her jacket and pulverized the glob with her teeth.

Bruna wanted to be a clockkeeper when she grew up. She had always been remarkable with time. At age six, she discovered clockkeeping in a library book of princess stories. In one of the tales, a princess escaped from her tormentor by fleeing to the local Church, where the priest concealed her identity by hiring her as the clockkeeper. When the king came to look for his imprisoned daughter, the priest lied to him, saying the princess had climbed up the clock tower at dawn and had taken her own life. The king trusted that the priest was telling the truth, and he built a marble statue of his lost daughter in the town square in her honor. For fifty years, the princess grew old in a tower of her own choice, oiling and coaxing the copper cogs morning, noon, and night.

In twelve years Bruna had never discovered another job that felt just right. Or more than right—real. Stable in reality, and essential for it. It was a shame that the job had peaked in the Middle Ages. There was a reason why obsolete jobs went away. Timekeeping was automated and nobody wanted to waste time checking the math. But why not? Bruna didn't understand. She valued her time so much, she desired a physical form for it. A body that relied on her care. She wanted to live in a lighthouse with a dome that housed a huge clock face. She wanted to cultivate the most well-oiled tick of a coastal clock—a vibration she would feel in her ribs more than her heartbeat. She wanted to grow chambers and valves that never stuttered with salt water, with gilded gears that outshone the house's glassy eye. She wanted to dedicate her routine and body to checking time. She wanted her routine to involve everyone's most primal routine. Saying yes or no to the exact moment the sun and moon were to emerge, down to one Mississippi. But it was useless to care about a fixture of the far past. Many human creations

—the children of mankind, with time being the eldest—had simply grown up and moved away, beyond their mother's care. Nostalgia would not bring them back.

Bruna crossed the street and checked her watch. She was now officially a minute late for work, which she had already decided was out of the question. She did not know where to go now, though. Home was an hour's walk through the sludge, and she didn't have a house key. She couldn't remember where her mother was going that morning. Thinking about how her mother didn't have her dream job either, she felt sad. Sad, but hopeful. Her mother had wanted to finish her biology PHD but had settled for a managerial position at the Juneau Museum of Science. That era had ended when Bruna was three—budget cuts—and Bruna's mother had started a surrogacy business. Fertility was a talent more than a learned skill, and Bruna's mother was naturally talented. Both Bruna and her older brother had absorbed their twins in the womb and had come out nine pounds or heavier. Now her mother was six months pregnant with her sixth batch of twins, set to be delivered to Sammi and Reed Swanton on the 14th of February. So her mother was probably halfway to Haines for an ultrasound or a mommy spa visit. But she didn't particularly want to go home, anyway. She was in a bad mood, feeling wronged on a cosmic level, and being outside already she would release her mood on the community rather than sulking it away.

She turned up a random street to avoid the wind tunnels by the river and found her surroundings strangely familiar. It was just a side street of pastel ranch houses like any other, but then she realized she was next to the home of one of her mom's former coworkers. She remembered tumbling around a screened front porch that housed a baby grand piano and a typewriter. When she looked up at the house, there they were: instruments of old, inside and outside simultaneously. The mailbox had the Juneau Science Museum logo on the front end, and the cursive name Dr. Amos Monroe on the side. She gasped and went onto the porch, unafraid.

She rang the doorbell and a monkey man answered. He was wearing a heavy down jacket, pinstriped slacks, and a pair of tortoise bifocals on his chimp body.

"You're soaked," said the monkey man, running his hand through his hair as though his head was wet as well. "What are you doing out there in the rain?"

"Doctor Monroe? I'm Monica Yehl's daughter. Bruna Yehl."

He oohed at her and clapped his hands. "I knew I recognized you! Remarkable. You were little the last time I saw you. All the more reason to come in, come in." He coaxed her out of the cold and shut the door.

"Remarkably, you remembered me, too," he said, pointing at her to sit on the sofa. A hologram of blue light ocean waves was simulating calm movement across the ceiling. She couldn't see its source projector anywhere in the room. The doctor poured two cups of tea and brought them to the coffee table.

"What brings you here, Bruna?" he said, sitting down. "Is it your mother? You know, I haven't seen her in a long time."

"I-I don't know. I suppose I recognized the piano on the porch."

He smiled. "Do you play?"

"No. I just...remembered it." She felt stupid. It seemed stupid to remember something so arbitrary from her childhood; to follow it so wholeheartedly. "I don't know."

"But you do know. Bruna, I'm afraid I remember you better than you remember yourself. When you were a little girl, you would force your mother and I to talk on the porch so you could play on the piano." He chuckled. "I had plenty of toys inside. But you were *obsessed* with the ivories. You were a special kid."

Bruna put her tea down. She had only remembered the vague sight of the instrument, like a faint beacon of light. Now the memory came rushing back: the smell of the rain on the porch, blended with the feeling of baby fingers and the sound of ears discovering a pure C note, like a sensorial smoothie.

"You remember, don't you?"

But she only had the one memory intact. "Vaguely."

"You were so young—barely three when I last saw you."

She looked around the room, trying to find her words. "Can I ask—what happened? I mean, I know my mom got fired. Laid off. But I don't remember why we stopped coming to see you."

Amos closed his eyes and smiled at the carpet. She discerned he felt forlorn, but the chimp was still smiling as always. "That's the thing, Bruna. Nothing has happened in the last fifteen years."

She was surprised by his sudden depressive tone; she almost giggled. "I don't—"

"Oh, I just mean that people drift away. Things change slowly, then all at once. Nothing happened between your mother and I. It was just easier to see each other when we worked together. When she left to start her own business, it was natural for the both of us to move on to the next stage in our lives. She was busy being a businesswoman and raising a toddler, or child, or teenager. And your mother wasn't fired—she was a genius, and still is a genius, and they had to lay her off for no reason other than money. But I do...I do feel she was cheated. Both of us did. And maybe it did drive something between us. It wouldn't feel right telling her about all the research and opportunities I've gotten at the Museum."

"I'm sure she would love to hear about them."

He chuckled. "I'm your godfather, you know."

She widened her eyes. "Really? I mean, I guess that makes sense, but—"

"You don't have to lie. It makes no sense at all. Yep, you don't hear much about godparents these days. But believe it or not, the two of us were in a church in the mid-2020s, and I was there watching you get drowned and cult-initiated. I have a photo on my fridge there."

She stood up and walked to the kitchen. "Which one of these women is my godmother?"

"You know—hell if I know. That is a question you'll have to ask Monica." He checked his watch. "I should be getting back to work soon."

"Oh, please don't let me keep you. It was so nice, you letting me in for tea. I haven't had tea in forever—"

"Bruna, I wasn't saying that so you'd leave. I was going to ask if you wanted to join me."

Bruna didn't know what to say. She didn't know what the hell Amos actually did for work. But she supposed she wouldn't mind wandering a museum while it rained.

"That is, if you don't have plans. You're not still in school, are you?"

"I just graduated in June. I'm supposed to be working, but I think I just quit my job."

"And how's that? Isn't that a coincidence—you've practically freed yourself up to work for me.'

Bruna laughed. "I have a job at the Super Target. But nobody else showed up for work this morning. Not my managers, not security, not anybody. Because of the storm, I guess? But all the lights were on, and the machines were on, too. *They* were working." She thought for a second. "I bet they're still working. I know what they're doing right this second. They're folding a pile of jeans, then unfolding them, then folding them again. For eternity. For no one."

"Bruna."

She cleared her throat. "Yes? Sorry."

"Can I tell you a secret? Actually, two secrets?"

"Yes." Bruna loved secrets. "I love secrets."

Amos stood up with a grin. "You got the endless curiosity of your mom." He walked over to the teapot and poured another cup. Then he went to the cupboard and topped the hot beverage with two shots of whiskey.

"The first secret," he said, "is that oolong and bourbon go together like chamomile and honey. Except they work together in the daytime. I don't celebrate the completion of a big project without it. Would you like some?"

"I don't see why not."

He took the bottle and a couple bourbon glasses and started leading her through the house. "We're going to the basement," he said.

She snorted. It was funny, zooming out on the situation: a young girl walking into the dark basement of a mad scientist chimp man. Maybe she should have been afraid, but she was the farthest thing from it.

"What's in the basement?"

"Good question. A very bright question, and an essential question to ask. You see, I don't do all my work at the Museum. To keep it short and sweet, not everything I am interested in doing gets approved there."

Now she was a little scared. "Like what?"

Amos started making his way down the dim stairs. "The Museum of Science does a lot of good work, believe me. But its biggest fault is believing it has limitations. Limitations concerning what science is allowed to be, and what funding will allow science to become. But I have decided to go beyond all that. I have the knowledge and the finances to do a lot of this myself. What's the acronym? D.I.Y."

"What is 'this'? I don't want to be rude, but I have to know what's down there before I go."

He sighed. "I'm concerned with Oxygenic Conservation. I'm creating a machine that preserves the element as it appears on Earth at its source. But I need humans to participate in its testing stage."

"Oxygenic...conservation?"

"Bruna. I want us to *breathe air*. Not just any air. *Real air*. Air at its source. Look—you know how all water has a certain taste. Tap water doesn't taste like spring water with naturally occurring minerals, bottled straight from the source. Air is like that, too. The air we breathe has a taste. The air in big cities is filtered through smog and exhaust, so much so that you can't get a full breath. Even the sound pollution is stored in the air you breathe. Your lungs can only fill about seventy-seven percent in the city of Boston; sixty-eight in New York. The air in urban areas is not like the air in rural areas. And the air in populated areas is nothing compared to the air in the

Sahara. But twenty-first-century air—do we even know what's in it? Do we even know if we're breathing "air" anymore? And does this new air have a different smell, a chemical profile poles apart to real air?"

"So you built a machine...that purifies the air? A fancy air purifier? I don't get it."

"It's not an air purifier—look, Bruna. For you to see *what* it is, I need to show you *how* it works. Are you ready?"

"Okay. Sure."

He smiled. "Are you sure you're not ready to walk back to Target?"

"Let's go downstairs."

"Let's go."

He flipped on the light switch. The basement had white walls, maroon shag carpeting, and a stack of labeled boxes in the corner. Other than that, the machine was the only thing in the room. It was a conjoined set of two orange, leather egg chairs. The back of the leather was caged in by four transparent legs that housed thousands of computer chips. The legs hooked over the sides of the twin chairs like an insect. Two white gas masks were plugged into the feet of the legs, and they sat unused on the orange cushions like virtual reality headsets.

"This is my machine," Amos said. "This is how we are going to become the first people in the twenty-first century to breathe real air. Air how it was before trains, planes, and automobiles. Air how it was...ante Christum natum."

"Doctor Amos. You're losing me. I think I'm even more confused than I was upstairs." She felt the orange leather. "Can I sit here?"

"Sit down and get comfortable." He sighed. "I'm overexplaining. Or jumping around the point. That is because I don't want you to be scared for your safety. I've tried this before with myself as the test subject and it's always been successful. Before that, I tested two hundred and seventeen squirrels and rats. All survived with this current model."

"You're going from confusing to bewildering."

"I'm talking about time travel, Bruna. I've created a time machine here."

Bruna looked back at the machine. She circled it, dumbfounded, observing every inch of the computer chip spider. She picked up the gas mask and stared into its insect eyes. "You created...a time machine...so you can... go back...and breathe?"

"It seems silly when you say it that way. But with a time machine, there isn't much else to do unless you want to kill the present as you know it. It's in your nature to want to be in control of the past, but you have to go against that. You have to be a passive observer. Don't talk to anybody; don't influence a flea. In the past, all you can do is breathe."

"Okay," Bruna said. "I think I'm starting to get it. We don't want to go back in time and create a paradox."

"Exactly. Well? Do you want to start?"

"What? Now? Go back in time?"

"Yeah. Go back in time," Amos said, with air quotes. "I would ask you if you're ready, but it's something you can't fully psychologically prepare for. But I believe you're ready, so that means that you are."

"Uhm," said Bruna.

"You know what I mean. Being 'ready' had nothing to do with it. You're standing in front of a time machine, Bruna. As far as I know, it's the only functioning time machine in the world. Will you use it to go back in time, Bruna?"

Bruna thought about how she was a secret clockkeeper. She was a clockkeeper who was still clocked in to another job somewhere across town. She was in a random basement instead, talking to her secret chimpanzee godfather.

"I want to go back in time," she said. "Can we take a shot first?"

* * *

Bruna's chest burned with a quirky bubble of fear. She had the urge to run, but was trapped in the retro chair. Amos had extended the side of a seatbelt from a pocket in the fabric, latching her in. He was still striding around the room with a notebook, presumably checking off a list of tasks. He flipped one of three switches under the banister, and the glass legs around the eggs began to hum with heat.

"What time do we set this thing to? Jurassic? Adam and Eve? I kinda need to know where we're going before we get there. For my safety. I haven't received a lot of preparation here, and I'd like to prepare."

Dr. Amos looked lost in thought for a moment. "You're safe. It's less of a time we're traveling to and more of a climate of air quality. The machine is programmed to choose a time and place on hospitable Earth that has the finest, freshest air quality. A time and place with zero, or hopefully negative, pollutants.

"*Negative* pollutants? What does that even mean? How does it know what air is the cleanest?"

"Lasers," he said. "They measure the air quality index."

"Don't you have a time frame?"

"Probably anywhere from 500 million years ago to 1750 C.E."

Her fear balloon started to fill.

"Relax. This thing won't land above water, or in climates below zero degrees Celsius. We're about to have a wonderful time. You won't want it to end, and you won't feel a thing."

Amos flipped the third light switch on the wall and the contraption began to vibrate, shifting into place like a dentist chair. He hopped into the egg to her left and strapped in. He flipped open a panel and brought an old keyboard into his lap, typing code into nowhere, or for a computer monitor she couldn't see.

"It won't hurt a bit," he said. "But you're going to want to close your eyes."

The whole room began to shake, but it was true; she acclimated easier with the bourbon in her system. She wrestled against the seatbelt, pressure on her pelvis like a vigorous rollercoaster ride, and she squeezed her eyes tight. She could die. Her body could die. She had not asked enough questions—mostly had knowledge sponged up from movies. Would her particles be rearranged? Was this time travel or universe-hopping? If she went to another universe, could she meet another version of herself? What if her future self from Universe Two traveled to her universe instead? If she had a time machine—a universe-hopper—then it made sense that other versions of herself would have one, too. Evil Brunas. It was too much to think of. No matter what Amos said, they would always influence the world with every action, including the choice to breathe in a given direction—breath had a weight to it, she knew because she felt how people flinched when air left her body because it would fall to the floor—and she opened her eyes. She spun faster than any amusement ride would allow, but she wasn't nauseous. Her eyes could not focus on the horizon or the destination but her body threw no tantrum; instead, her brain was preoccupied with the fact that its vision was infinitely mirrored and upside down. Her vision began fragmenting like bug eyes and moving off in cell fragments, trying to find the visual identification of nonsense particles from their home in reality. She became afraid, thinking that her ocular cells might not make their way back to her in time. They could be lost in this middle ground, and she would not be able to see. But then the landscape cooled like lava, like the heat death of the universe, and so did her eyes. She saw a memory of herself in the car with her mom, driving away from the screened-in porch in the rain. Then she could feel her feet again, on pins and needles. She could picture herself standing up; seeing herself in a mirror.

She squeezed her eyes shut and took a shuddery breath. All she kept thinking was she was alive. She couldn't believe it.

"Amos," she said. She unlatched her belt and fell like a bag of sand in the grass, knocking the wind out of her. She could barely feel her limbs, and the tips of her fingers were shriveled and white.

"I'll admit—that was a bit of a rockier landing. Two humans at once—it's never done two humans at once."

"Don't tell me that yet. We still have to go back," she said.

"That numb feeling will go away after a minute."

Bruna pressed her buzzing fingers into a fist, feeling the long grass on her back. Amos brought the keyboard back down and typed in a long code. A window opened on the roof of the left egg, and a blue laser popped out, which scanned a nearby tree like a sprinkler.

"Here's the fun part for you, Bruna. You get to know exactly where and when we are."

Finally, she thought. She would get off the ground with the certainty that there were no dinosaurs. The blue laser slowly dissipated and the window slid shut. On the left side of the left egg was a tiny monitor, almost like the radio in her grandpa's old truck, and it slowly displayed three sets of blinking numbers and letters. Amos wrote these hastily in his notebook.

"Calculated GPS coordinates, month/day/year, ancient or modern," he said. "I have all these acronyms decoded somewhere in here...ah! Pangea. This is modern-day Santarém, Brazil, by the looks of it.

"Pangea? Brazil? Christ. There aren't dinosaurs here, are there?"

"It's the year 224 million before Christ," he said. "November 3rd, 224,535,003 B.C.E. Of course there are dinosaurs."

"Fuck. Fucking hell. What have I gotten myself into—"

"Bruna. The same principle still stands. We get in, we get out without disturbing any living thing. The dinosaurs won't even know we're here."

Bruna looked at him dumbfounded. "Dinosaurs aren't *people*, Amos. Do you hear yourself? A T-Rex will eat you if it smells you from a mile away. Eat *us*."

He wasn't hearing her. "The air here is the most pure it has ever been in all of history, Bruna. Santarém is where the Tapajós meets the Amazon River. The meeting of these two rivers makes this a very fertile place. Look at this reading—it's coming up as *negative thirteen* AQI. That shouldn't even be possible by modern standards. The air here is so clean..." he paused to take a deep breath. His nostrils flared and he exhaled like a newborn waking up on its first morning alive.

"...I mean, can you smell it? Nobody has smelled clean air like this for almost three hundred years. Take it all in, Bruna. Here. Close your eyes again. Just breathe for a moment, before those pesky dinosaurs eat us."

She laid back down in the tall grass to humor him and closed her eyes. She inhaled until her lungs were filled, and then inhaled some more. She felt the crystals of deep breath wash over her insides, filling her stomach and heart with nutrients. It was air that tasted like she crawled out of bed at dawn and had snorted the dew off a rose with both nostrils. The grass inhaled alongside her when she pinched its locks between her fingers.

"It tastes like water," she said. She hadn't noticed it before when the air had been knocked out of her lungs. She had been preoccupied. "It's filling."

"Exactly. Now you understand?"

Even in Alaska, she had never smelled fresh air like this before. Nothing could compare. Not the air around the St. Therese Shrine during her Junior High retreat (the most nowhere she had ever been). Not the air in the Gulf of Alaska, when she had taken that cruise with her grandpa. Her grandfather's grandfather had not known air like this. It had all been tainted by something small yet persistent in her memory. A mosquito of exhaust had been eternally present in these places; a booger in her nostril. Amos was right. She had never breathed real air.

She became emotional, like the long green was tickling her tear ducts. She felt choked up. If she could just have this—the comfort of breathing deeply, nourishingly—air that not only prolongs life, but invigors it?

She felt her lungs telling her that they had incurred an oxygen debt. Her habitual behavior had seriously damaged her lung score. But, not to worry—she could pay off any outstanding corporal payments in due time, if only she stayed here. And the clearing was, in fact, dinosaurless for the time being. She trusted her godfather

—this strange monkey man who had brought her somewhere like heaven. He would get her in, get the air, and get out.

"The Triassic," Amos said. "Of course it's here. The age of reptiles...giants growing larger by the hour, down by the river. Rivers. Air here is protein-rich, like the soil. Warm-blooded creatures growing like sunflowers. Tell me, Bruna...would you hate it if we stayed here?"

She sat up in the grass. He was leaning against the roof of the contraption with his arms folded, scanning the area. He was serious. She wanted him to take a moment to lie down in the grass beside her. She found the greenery so thick and fluid that it was bobbing her up and down like ocean water. It was less disorienting than Amos' contemplation.

"What did you just say?"

"Suppose if we stayed here and lived here. Mankind —twenty-first-century mankind—hasn't gotten a chance to develop under these natural conditions. What would life be like if you were healed by the air you breathe? What would it be like to be nourished constantly? The air back home...once you've been here, it's not the same. You realize the world taxes your breath. And it makes it hard to go through with it. Breathing."

Bruna remembered the inconsequential memory that had come to her in the time machine: her mother, her in the car seat, driving away. She wanted to drive away from this moment. But cars and wheels did not exist in the mind of this second universe.

"I think that's fundamentally flawed," she said. "Haven't people developed better in modern times? Modern healthcare? Long lifespans? Clean bedding? It might be in our nature to breathe here, but we sure as hell weren't nurtured to. It's nice to think about, but we couldn't actually thrive here. Eventually, we'll want to go back. Right?"

She swallowed a lump in her throat. "Right, Amos? Have you been here before? This spot?"

"No, no. This is the best reading I've ever gotten. First time programming the machine for the greatest possible oxygen results in the database. In my first twenty experiments, I only sent pairs of rodents. Never more than two. The machine sent them to a bunch of different places and times, all before the current era: Nome, Alaska; Mesopotamia and Madagascar. They all came back happy and healthy, if not a little numb like you were. The first time I went by myself, I went to Santiago, Chile. Not too far from here, hypothetically. 35.2 percent of the time, I've gone to prehistoric South America. Maybe I've just been getting closer and closer to the perfect spot. Negative thirteen AQI."

"Why never more than two at a time?"

"Well...the machine gets overwhelmed handling more than two nervous systems. I only tried a group of guinea pigs once. Their spines and brain tissue came back fused. But it's nothing to worry about. There are only two of us. If you were pregnant, you wouldn't have drunk my bourbon."

She looked at him, horrified. She had been in denial about any of this being unsafe. No matter her primal fears, she was stuck; she might as well keep trusting him. She thought everything he said was slightly more fantastical and tinfoil hat—she was time traveling with a monkey mad scientist, after all—and the only thing on his radar was this crazy obsession with capturing the cardinal component of life: breath. What a silly thing to care about, breathing debt. She had lived eighteen years of her life in a city—so what? Had it really taken a toll on her way of life *that much*, if her lungs were still breathing automatically?

She turned to her companion. "You don't want to go back, do you? You found real air, and now you want me to go back without you." She laughed, dumbfounded.

"*That's* the only reason why you took me here, isn't it? I'm your time-traveling Uber driver. I showed up on your porch, and you thought: it's a sign from God. It's time to move."

Finally, he came down from the machine and sat cross-legged in the grass. He petted the heads of the stalks and breathed deeply.

"Stop breathing, goddammit," Bruna yelled. "I know I'm right."

"It's not that I wanted to break us apart. In time, in space. This reunion between us—it's been so special to me. It's not that I don't want to go back. If I go back, I won't be able to forget this feeling. It's not replicable. I know you feel it when you breathe. The tax, Bruna. You're not even taking a fraction of the breaths you're supposed to. There's smog when you can't see it; exhaust when you can't smell it. It's in one hundred percent of the air back in 2042. In 2042, Bruna—as a scientist—I can confidently say that I have no idea what you are breathing. Is the air oxygen? Maybe if Kool-Aid is water."

Bruna started to cry. She leaned over with her knees on her stomach and let her tears hit the dirt. She heard Amos coo and felt his warm hand press on her back. She wanted so desperately to hug her mother, clinging to her shoulders, but her mind reminded her that her mother did not exist, would not exist maybe ever in this universe, and she was paralyzed knowing that all that was familiar was fiction here.

"You clearly have no clue," she sniffled, "how it would feel to abandon you here. To go back alone."

He tilted his head. "It's not—you're not abandoning me. That's not how I feel here. Being here would save me. I would have my freedom back."

"But what about your life? We all have lives back home. Things you care about."

"He laughed. Of course I have a life. I have an extremely successful career. I'm self-published. I have an ex-wife; extended family. I have you, Bruna, and your mother. But having *a life* is not the same as *living*. This is the last invention that I wanted to make. This was my life's purpose."

She felt nauseous. "You're talking crazy again," she said. "And my mom—you don't even see her anymore. Is that why she stopped talking to you? Letting you around me? Because...because you do *things* like *this*?"

Amos looked down at the dirt. "I don't—I don't know."

Bruna stood up and wiped her eyes with a soiled hand. "I'm not just leaving you here alone. There are things you'll miss about your life. People. Here's some science for you: people need to socialize to be happy. What's your plan? Are you just going to talk to yourself forever? Until you get stomped to death by dinosaurs?"

"Who said that I had fulfilling experiences *socializing* back home?" he put the word in air quotes. "This isn't my suicide, Bruna. This is the only thing I want. I told you: back home, I cannot breathe."

He was dead serious. He had conned her into this plan. And she thought: was she the crazy one? Was she selfish for not letting him disappear into the distant past? There was no way. He wasn't prepared for this. He would die in an instant. And she would be haunted forever by the fact that she had let him die.

"I know you think I'm not prepared for this," he said. "That I am doomed to die. But you do not know. Just like you didn't think any of this was possible. You just do not know."

"Amos," she said. She saw that he was crying, and she reached for his hand.

"It isn't made for me," he cried. "You can't tell me I'm not at home here. You can't tell me that the air back there is wrong."

"I'm sorry," she said, and she was crying too. She was grasping at straws. How could she fulfill a primal need for him, a need like blood or sleep or water, an elemental nutrient that had already gone extinct? She could not understand what he was feeling—and yet, when she thought about herself she saw her true self that spent her days clock cleaning and timekeeping, locked away in a sunlit attic to ponder the most elementary things, not the girl who was still clocked in at the Juneau Super Target.

"Can't we take it back with us? I don't know...a single air canister. A jar. A fucking pool floatie. Anything we can fill."

"The cells that make up an air canister will reformat themselves in transport, and they will eat twenty-first-century air. As soon as you get back home, your mitochondria start collecting fake air. To put it short, it will be tainted. Even if it wasn't tainted, it wouldn't last."

"So there's nothing I can do. No way we can bring the air back."

"Even if we could, how would it last? One canister versus the entire atmosphere. It would be like...the world's most wonderful inhaler. But no, it wouldn't last; wouldn't compare. *That* would make me suicidal. No, Bruna. I know what I want."

"Can't you take the time machine back whenever you want?"

"It doesn't...quite work like that." He cleared his throat. "The 'time-machine' as you know it is a literary device conceived by H.G. Wells. I can't exact the same coordinates twice. The machine chooses, except to go back to the point of origin. And it's not traveling back in time, exactly. We are in a timeline where 224 million B.C.E. co-occurs with our own dimension, 2042 C.E.. Isn't that—"

"I know how the multiverse theory works. They made time-travel movies after the eighties." She furrowed her brow. "And you could have told me *exactly* what the fuck I was getting into before you went around *rearranging my particles.*"

"The universes are arranged in a stack of cubes, like dominoes," he said. "When we 'time-travel', we cultivate enough energy to propel through the membrane of our universe, connecting our 'domino' to the next domino. Sometimes the second falls against a third, and a fourth. We just keep colliding and colliding through infinite possibilities of membranes," he said. He was separating a piece of grass down the center. "Bruna. I'm sorry about how I've made you feel today. Do you want to breathe with me one more time?"

"You should know," she said, "That this experience has been a curse rather than a blessing."

He frowned. "I could imagine seeing it that way. It's a grand experience. Certainly one that's out of your comfort zone."

She grit her teeth. "You're asking me to choose between this air and everything else. You chose this place over *everything else*." Over me, she thought.

He scratched at his head, monkeylike. "I suppose... the right choice comes easier to some than others."

"Fuck you." She turned around and trudged back to the egg. She realized she didn't even know how to direct the contraption.

"It's not just air, Bruna." He sounded like her mother. Chiding. She started to ugly cry.

"Did you even give yourself a second to breathe? Or were you too busy thinking?"

She buckled her own seatbelt. This time, she sat in Amos' egg on the left. She did not look up at her godfather as she struggled to open the keyboard compartment. She finally lowered the old thing and wiped her nose on her sleeve so she wouldn't leave any snot on the mask.

"Bruna. Wait."

Amos stood up and walked over to her. A large breeze blew a wave of blue wind through her senses. He lifted up the right seat cushion, apparently used for storage, and took out an empty water bottle with a sippy cup straw. He unscrewed the top and held the container up to the wind, latching it quickly after another wave whistled into its center.

"A gift, from me to you," he said. "Don't think about this anymore. Time doesn't work like you think, Bruna. I'll be alive where and when it matters most to me."

"But you'll be impossible to reach. Physics won't account for it. You will be in the past, forever. From where I am—from my twenty-first-century *mind*, Amos—you are dead in the ground somewhere. Isn't that—traumatizing?"

He sighed. "You already forgot this isn't the universe you know. This isn't *the* past but a replica of the past. A nostalgic world, realized."

"Nostalgia," she scoffed. "And yet you never got to experience what this was like the first time around."

"My atoms did," he said. "But you'll miss that point, too. Go, baby girl. Key in CTRL>SHIFT>PRTSC>4. Close your eyes and think. The machine is connected to your nervous system—*don't* overthink *that*. The point is: it will take you wherever you truly want to go."

He smiled. "Maybe this isn't real to you, Bruna. But something out there is real to you."

Maybe untouched, ungoverned reality, she thought, wanting to say it out loud, but then she remembered the jeans-folding robots. Nostalgia prison or robots? Robots, or nostalgia prison? Was any of this real? She was starting to get a headache.

She took a hurried breath and typed in the key. The machine started to whir.

"Goodbye, Amos," she said. "I do love you. And find shelter and water before nightfall."

He smiled. "Not my first rodeo," he said. "I love you, too, Bruna. You've been the best assistant of my career. And give all my love to Monica."

Bruna gasped for the sweet air at the sound of her mother's name as she spun into pure darkness, but it had already evaporated. She squeezed her eyes shut until she could feel her heartbeat in her eyeballs. Her mind was spinning faster than her body. The machine relied on her: it would not know where to go without her direction. But where did she want to go the most? She was more confused than ever, and could not make a conscious choice in this place and time, between leaving and entering. Her eyelids fluttered with endless memories baked in a vacuum oven: snippets of her mother waving goodbye in the parking lot, of old cracked book spines at the library. Every wish her heart conceived received blowback from her mind, which knew whatever place she selfishly traveled to would be a mirrored reality, separated from all she once knew. She could not go where she wanted because it would not be as real as she had dreamt. Her heart leaped at the idea of swinging the machine back to the point of origin, kidnapping her mother, and bringing her to a seventeenth-century Parisian clock tower, where they could live like clockwork, like copper and gold, just like her favorite story. She wanted to cry for that little girl in the library, who knew what she wanted but would never be able to receive it. That dream could not be born into human hands. Though realistic to herself, it could not be realized.

Her heart turned like an autumn leaf. Only one memory was sticking with her, perhaps as residue from leaving Amos, and that was the snippet of her, three years old in the backseat, driving away from the piano porch in the rain. Her mother's hair was turning, too, barely grey fifteen years ago. It glinted gold and silver in the red prism of downpours and stoplights. She remembered the calm of her mother being at the steering wheel: how she would smile whenever Bruna told a joke. If she had it again, it would not light up her heart with gold the way it did now. The past. That was where she wanted to go. But if she went there, she would not be herself at three. And her mother would be a replica from another dimension—a poor imitation. So she did not want it at all. No. She wanted...she wanted...a world without ears. A world that did not alter itself for anyone. These thoughts spiraled, photographs of memories flipping by like they were loose and lost to the surrounding darkness. She smiled. Once she opened her eyes, she would not be anywhere in particular. She would just be.

Who?

After retiring from a long and successful career as a software developer and technical architect, **David Castlewitz** turned to a first love: writing fiction, particularly SF, fantasy, magical realism, and light horror. His stories have appeared in many anthologies and online as well as print publications. David lives on the North Shore, outside Chicago, where he enjoys long walks, the occasional bike ride, and other outdoor adventures.

Casey Richards-Bradt is a horror and science fiction writer who has studied at Emerson College. They love tankas and Tim O'Brien. You can find their other work at Reader Beware Magazine and The Piker Press.

James Dick is an actor, author, screenwriter, director, and former fossil smuggler who remains on Parks Canada's "Most Wanted" list. In 2024, he graduated from Toronto Metropolitan University with a B.A. in Media Studies and is still trying to figure out what to do with it. Every December, he grows pointy ears and works as Santa's elf, but is frequently mistaken for a Vulcan. He lives in Toronto, Ontario.

www.ingramcontent.com/pod-product-compliance
Lightning Source LLC
LaVergne TN
LVHW010405070526
838199LV00065B/5898